Knit One Girl Two
&
Fearless
by Shira Glassman

plus:
"Your Name is Love"
Complete bonus story by Shira Glassman
Included as a teaser
for the Mangoverse series

a collection of romances between women about reconnecting with art, music, & inspiration

This is a work of fiction. Names, characters, places, and incidents are either the product of the author's imagination or are used fictitiously, and any resemblance to any persons, cats, roseate spoonbills, snakes, scorpions, conchs, or hermit crabs, living or dead, business establishments, events, or locales is entirely coincidental.

Knit One, Girl Two by Shira Glassman, edited by J.L. Douglas

Small-batch independent yarn dyer Clara Ziegler is eager to brainstorm new color combinations--if only she could come up with ideas she likes as much as last time! When she sees Danielle Solomon's paintings of Florida wildlife by chance at a neighborhood gallery, she finds her source of inspiration. Outspoken, passionate, and complicated, Danielle herself soon proves even more captivating than her artwork...

Cover art by Jane Dominguez

Fearless by Shira Glassman, edited by Jaymi Lynn

Lana Novak hasn't played violin in over twenty years, her musical life these days confined to being a devoted band mom to her clarinet whiz daughter Robin. She didn't think she could get back into it after this long, but Melanie Feinberg, the outgoing, enthusiastic, and very cute butch orchestra director from Robin's school, has other ideas.

Art by Caroline C. and Jane Dominguez

Acknowledgements

J.L. Douglas for editing
Áine Noonan for proofing
Jane, Shermi, and especially Caitlin for
indie dyer technical help and ideas
Ducky, Kat, & Kate for reading early drafts
Erin and Mehek for beta-reading
Ellie Blair and Lyssa Bowen for answering
questions about the work side of art
Marina for inspiration
Ginger for guidance on Lyme Disease
K.D. Lubeck and Xan West for guidance on
trans and fat characters; all remaining
errors mine
Eliana for a second pair of eyes on kashrut
Vee from GayYA who named the
nonbinary kid
Greg for not killing me for using his name.
We the musicians appreciate you.
Erik, Eponine, and Johanna: *If I cannot fly,
let me sing!*
Roseate spoonbills for existing
Gayle for verifying the large print format

and

Mehek Naresh again, for the sprint that got me off my writing drought

Contents:

Notes for *Knit One Girl Two*:

According to the staff, the Museum of Discovery and Science no longer has a goliath grouper, so the "Jewfish" sign I remember from my adolescence is not there in real life.

References to characters from my other contemporaries are intentional

for Caitlin,
who keeps the lights on.

Knit One, Girl Two

"So you're doing sock club again?" Jasmine Ziegler asked, making tinkly noises on her coffee cup with long electric-blue nails.

"I really want to," said her older sister Clara, "but, like." She paused. "I'm afraid I used all my best ideas on the first go-round. All that time I was planning and practicing, I was also narrowing down my colors. Only the best made it in, and that means I...kinda used up my best."

"No problem," said Jasmine. "Just means you have to start from scratch and come up with six more best ideas!"

"Yeah, I know." Clara sipped her apple cider. "I think I'm suffering from the perfect being the enemy of the good, though. Like, my first round got *such* positive feedback so now I'm like, what if I can't do that again? I can't be less picky, but..."

"I wonder if anyone's ever drawn that."

"What?"

"The perfect being the enemy of the good," said Jasmine. "Like superheroes."

"Which one's the villain?" asked Clara.

"Perfect," they agreed at the same time.

"But he's not *bad* bad," Jasmine continued. "It could be like one of those 'good guys fighting each other' storylines the comics are always doing to get more attention."

"Perfect never has a bad hair day." Clara squinted to count the stitches on her knitting needle.

"Good's wearing socks that don't match, but he always holds the door open for little old ladies," Jasmine added enthusiastically.

"Perfect's cat is toilet trained."

Jasmine burst out laughing. "I'm writing this down. You could use it in the sock club."

Just then, an older woman in a business suit stopped by their table. "I'm sorry, did you say sock club?" Clara nodded enthusiastically. "What's that?"

"I dye yarn," Clara explained, "in my kitchen. I dyed this, actually!" She held up her project, which was light pink, varying shades of plum, and navy blue.

"Ooh, very nice!"

"Sock club is this thing a lot of indie dyers—sorry, independent, small-batch dyers—are doing where you pay a flat fee and every month or every other month you get a surprise yarn color."

"My brother gave us something like that for Christmas last year, only it was gourmet food from around the world," said the stranger.

"I've seen those," said Jasmine. She thwapped Clara's upper arm. "That's where I got so obsessed with dried goldenberries. From Dana's food thing. It was in the Peruvian themed box."

"Basically like that," Clara agreed. "A lot of us also include little free treats with the yarn, like handmade soap, or stitch markers."

"What a neat idea!" said the woman.

"Are you interested?" Clara beamed, rummaging around in her purse for a business card.

But by the time she had it out, the woman held up her hand. "Oh, no thanks, I don't knit. I don't have the patience." She smiled and continued past them out of the café.

"If you had a dollar for every time you heard that," Jasmine remarked.

"Out of all the things people say," said Clara, "that's the one I understand the least. I don't have the patience *not* to! I mean, I totally get it when people try it and don't like it because their fingers won't do the thing. But I'm already sitting here. I'm already watching TV. I'm already hanging out with people. Why shouldn't I have something in my hands taking shape while I'm doing it?"

"They probably mean they don't have the patience to start something that takes so long to finish," Jasmine pointed out, "but don't look at me—I'm the girl who started from scratch and sewed an entire dress during a *Star Wars* marathon."

"And you've been a legend for it since college." Clara grinned.

"I bet you could do something like that, knit a pair of socks during *Lord of the Rings*, or something," Jasmine suggested. "To help get publicity for Sock Club Round Two."

"Do I really need publicity at this point?" asked Clara. "I had twenty-five people in the first round."

"You might be able to get it up to fifty! Especially since you've got the pictures from last time now."

"I don't know if I could handle fifty," said Clara. "And in any case, I need ideas first."

Daydreaming about color combinations was never far from Clara's brain over the next few days. During her commute she watched the dance of the other cars on the road — lots of reds, grays, black, golds, silvers—constantly shifting and shimmering. In the box office, and in the theater's hallway just outside, she studied the posters and cast photos for shows gone by. A riot of colors to rival any art supply store gave her every combination possible, but they didn't really work as sock yarn.

I bet if I did one themed on musicals, she mused to herself, *the theater nerds would snap it up.* But would they *look* any good?

It was one thing in theory, but producing an attractive *sock* was the goal at the end of the day, not just 'sounding cool.' Some of the most iconic and memorable musicals had posters that wouldn't produce stand-out socks, once you teased out their basic color scheme.

She was thinking particularly of Les Miz.

"I don't have any more seats together in the first ten rows," she said apologetically to her customer as she forced her brain out of the dye-pot. "I could either put you one behind the other in rows six and seven, or together in row fourteen."

Clara took her lunch break at two, giving the audience members on more conventional lunch schedules time to get back to their office jobs. "Taco truck?" she called to Nasreen as she slipped her purse strap over her shoulder.

Her coworker shook her head and waved a plastic container at her. "Leftovers. Thanks, though! No, wait, can you bring me back a Gatorade?"

"Any particular flavor?"

"Anything but yellow."

Clara stepped out into the harsh Florida sunshine, blinking a couple of times as her eyes got used to not being in the office. It was slightly worse just outside the theater because the Intercoastal Waterway was right there, twinkling reflected sunlight.

She had an hour. If she hurried, she had time to wander around the shops and galleries before she was due back at work. The more diverse images she provided for her hungry brain, the better the chances of inspiration.

Clara obtained her pair of tacos from the man in the shiny green truck and ate them quickly by the riverside. Nearby, a saxophone player serenaded people sitting outside for a late lunch in one of the fancier restaurants in the area, and a boat full of tourists passed by, ready to gawk at the homes of the rich.

She hopped up when she was done, in search of Nasreen's Gatorade. The first place she looked was the pizza parlor, but, as she had feared from Nasreen's instructions, all they had was lemon-lime. Glancing at her watch, she kept walking, figuring she had plenty of time.

Clara headed into the area with shops and galleries, figuring a convenience store would pop up, well, conveniently!

Instead, she found modern art, expensive shoes, a store devoted entirely to pet supplies that looked more well-made than half her wardrobe, and horribly garish handbags. Well, she definitely knew what she *didn't* want her next sock club to look like.

She crossed to the next street. Oh, good, there was a bodega across the way. Just then, a beautiful nude sculpture caught her attention in the window of the gallery she was nearest.

"I am so gay," she whispered to herself happily. It was just your ordinary classical nude, probably a Muse or something, but it was curvy and well-made and it put a smile on her face.

But as she looked beyond the sculpture into the gallery itself, she found herself intrigued by the paintings she saw beyond. Their subjects weren't unusual for Ft. Lauderdale—mostly familiar Florida scenes. Vivid pinks and greens and gold contrasted with mild blues and greys, as coconut palms and roseate spoonbills interacted with sunset or stormy backgrounds.

She moved from painting to painting, licking bits of cilantro out of her teeth but barely blinking. Here was a mango tree; there a plumeria in full bloom. Here more roseate spoonbills, their strange beaks instantly recognizable even if their pink feathers weren't already enough.

It was something about the intensity level the artist had chosen, or maybe it was the way they'd combined their colors. Either way, whatever it was, Clara was hooked. This was it. This was the perfect theme for her next sock club.

Images of promotional posts, featuring the most inspiring paintings, flashed into her mind. Maybe she could do some mini-interviews with the artist, about how they chose their scenes, or if they'd had any fun adventures while taking reference photos.

It all, of course, depended on the person's consent! Maybe they'd be weirded out by the whole idea. Maybe they'd want too much of a cut to make it worthwhile— kettle-dying yarn in small batches was a lot of labor. Maybe they'd think it was too nerdy or too grandmotherly for their high-class image.

Clara, however, was not the kind of person to let these thoughts stand in her way. "Excuse me — whose paintings are these?" she asked the gallery attendant.

"Right now we're displaying Danielle Solomon, and the statue in the window is by Xavier Jurado. Do you need me to spell that?"

"No thanks, I was just interested in the paintings. Would I be able to get in touch with Ms. Solomon online?"

"She does have a website," said the attendant, "but she's authorized us to handle all sales."

"It's..." Clara geared up for the impending awkwardness. "It's not so much about sales. I was interested in a... sort of a collaboration..." She took her unfinished sock out of her purse and then handed him a business card. "I dye yarn."

"Yarn?"

"Small-batch luxury hand-dyes. Merino, usually. Or merino-nylon, or merino-nylon-cashmere..." She realized she was tiptoeing the 'crank' line and dialed it back. "I'm interested in making these paintings the inspiration for my next—uh, my next yarn line." There, that sounded more like fashion and she wouldn't have to explain sock clubs to someone who was clearly skeptical of her right to claim artistic talent.

"Well, I'll leave this for her and she can get in touch with you if she's interested." His tone was dismissive as he placed Clara's business card on his desk.

"Thank you," said Clara, smiling through her total lack of optimism.

Oh, well, she thought as she left the gallery and hurried across the street for the Gatorade. If inspiration could come that strongly, it was still out there somewhere else, right?

Clara flipped the switch on her crock-pot and settled into her squishy sofa with her laptop. She had three hours before

Jasmine got home from OasisLand, so hopefully the cookbook wasn't lying about this recipe's prep time. Crock-pots still seemed vaguely magical to her.

The Phantom jumped up beside her and aggressively headbutted her thigh. "Sorry, we don't have any more front-row seats," she said in what Jasmine called her "Creepy Cat Mom" voice while mock-nombling his head. He tried again to push her laptop out of the way. "Oh, my *God*."

They eventually compromised, with the laptop on one leg and the cat on the other, his paws folded under his head as if he were contemplating deep things.

She pulled up the Captain Werewolf page on a fanfiction site to check for new uploads and quickly got engrossed in a story where he and his team saved all the Deco buildings on South Beach from sea monsters. Breezing through the adventure, she soon clicked the link for Chapter Four, only to get an error message. Sure enough, the site's Twitter account verified that they were having a momentary hiccup. "Yaaaay, just when I get home." The Phantom looked up at her with alarm at the outburst, then resumed his pose of maximum chill.

They said they expected to be back online any minute, so she opened another tab and found herself searching the artist from the gallery showing. Danielle Solomon wasn't too hard to find, and her website was slick and professional. Clara recognized the same Florida brightness in the pictures online, though except for one coconut palm they looked like different ones from the ones she'd seen earlier.

She clicked 'About' while narrowly missing closing the tab entirely, thanks to The Phantom demanding scritches by inserting his forehead where he clearly thought it belonged.

The page started with an artist's statement. ***Everyone is out there trying to get likes these days. My art is me clicking Like on G-d's Instagram. I'm filled with enthusiasm for my subjects, and it overflows beyond my body into my paintings and sketches. That being said, I believe in craft as much as self-expression, and strive to accurately reproduce the beauties of the world as I perceive them.***

Clara's eyes glazed over the where-she-went-to-school parts and landed on the photo at the bottom, beside a digital reproduction of Danielle Solomon's swoopy illegible signature.

She was momentarily shocked by how attractive she looked— whatever Clara had expected wasn't this curvaceous brunette beauty. Between Danielle Solomon's zaftig figure, flowy shirt, and the gentle way her black curls cascaded around her face, she seemed to Clara an ideal from an earlier age. Surely she'd seen people going for that look in various theater productions.

The effect was enhanced by the thoughtful romance of Danielle's expression, not smiling but not unhappy.

She looked, Clara decided, like a Jewish Snow White. *With a treyf apple*, she joked to herself as she closed the tab, self-conscious about the awkwardness of her sudden reaction.

Danielle Solomon: very cute, very talented, and probably in very different circles from little nobody Clara Ziegler. Danielle was someone people Had Heard Of; she was in a gallery in a street where Clara could only afford Gatorade, and the people who had money enough to buy her paintings were those who kept the lights on in the theater, not sold the tickets. Clara figured she could always try to scavenge more about her as a person instead of professionally on Facebook, but there was such a thing as being a creeper.

Clara retrieved her current sock project and maximized the tab in which she'd been watching Captain Werewolf. It didn't take long to completely absorb her attention—in her own way, of course. She found herself staring down every interesting camera shot for potential color combinations, as usual.

She was murmuring to The Phantom, "There's gotta be a way to get *exactly that copper*," in response to Captain Werewolf's sidekick's red hair when her phone rang. It was too early for Jasmine to be out, so her adrenaline level rose slightly just as it did for any unexpected phone call. Her grandfather—

It wasn't Mom on the phone, though, but an unfamiliar local number. "Hello?"

"Hey, is this Clara from *Ft. Sockerdale Knitworks*?"

"Speaking?"

"This is Danielle Solomon. Tucker at the gallery texted me a picture of your card—"

"Oh my gosh, yes!" Clara blinked rapidly and slammed her laptop shut. The Phantom sprang away in disdain and went off to lick his paw in the middle of the kitchen floor.

"He said something about you wanting to do a yarn line based on my paintings," said Danielle.

"Yeah," said Clara. "I'm a small-batch indie dyer, and I was really inspired by what I saw today." She explained how sock clubs worked. "So, there would be six of them, spread out over a year."

"And people don't know what they're getting beforehand?"

"Nope!" Clara said brightly. "For a lot of them, that's the appeal. And many of us, we make it exclusive so that if you don't sign up and you see how pretty the color is once we get to that month, too bad so sad."

"Ah, that's how you get 'em." Danielle chuckled.

"I mean, it's not for everybody," Clara continued. "My friend Marisol is super picky about colors so she never does sock club because the surprise doesn't make sense for her."

"Wouldn't people be able to get spoilers from my website, though?"

"That's on them. Besides, it's not like *they* know what I'm going to do with all the shades of pink in a roseate spoonbill. I could do... variegated, speckles, semisolids with a contrasting heel-toe color..."

"Yeah, I was looking at your website," said Danielle. "I don't know how to knit, but I loved what I saw. The colors believed in themselves."

Clara beamed. "Ooh, I like that. Can I use it as a testimonial?"

Danielle giggled again. "Sure. Speaking of which, we should get together and discuss the legal stuff."

"Oh, sure!" sure Clara. Thinking quickly of the bleeped-out "o" in "God" on Danielle's website, she steered her suggestion towards something more compatible with a stricter observance than hers, just in case. "Are you free for lunch Sunday? We could go to the Deli Den." There. Addictive kosher food *and* not interrupting Shabbat.

"Sounds great! Don't let me hog the half-sours."

"Thumb-wrestle you for them," Clara blurted, before flushing at her forwardness. Ugh, why did her game sound like she was thirteen?

"No way, with you knitting all the time you probably have super-fingers," said Danielle. "How about one o'clock?"

"Okay, cool!"

As Clara hung up the phone, she stood there blinking into the empty house. For a moment she felt like she were trying to reconcile two Danielles — the gorgeous stranger on the website, and the friendly real person on the phone who was also in all statistical likelihood, straight. *I'm just making a friend, is all*, she told herself.

But then she saw that picture in her mind again, the vintage beauty of her, and grinned in spite of herself.

"I figured out the next sock club."

"Oh, cool!" Jasmine swished the ladle through the crock pot, most likely aiming for the unattainable ideal of an equal ratio of goodies. "What is it?"

Clara explained about the gallery. "So we're meeting for lunch on Sunday."

She wouldn't have realized how transparent she was if Jasmine hadn't countered with, "I've known what that look means ever since I first saw it at Daniel Greenbaum's bar mitzvah reception, when you and that band girl, Lauren or whatever—"

Heat flared in Clara's cheeks and she covered her grin with one hand. "Memories, man. Why do *you* remember that?"

"You were gone for like a half hour," said Jasmine. "In twelve-year-old years that's an eternity."

"That was a good eternity," mused Clara as she ate.

"So anyway," said Jasmine. "This artist?"

Clara smiled as she shook her head. "I'm just havin' fun. She looked super cute on her website, but she's probably straight."

Sunday afternoon at five minutes to one found Clara sitting in the parking lot of the Deli Den, primping. Not that it *mattered* mattered, but there was no sense in not looking her best for the first time meeting a new work contact, either. She made a flamboyant kissy face at her reflection — straight dark brown hair, small dark eyes under well-sculpted brows, a prominent nose, and a killer smile. Beyond the mirror's reach was a tailored shirt in plum plaid and a brown skirt.

Jasmine had called her out on the plaid that morning. "Just in case?"

Clara only stuck her tongue out.

Time for the meeting! She scooped up her pile of sketches and printouts and left the car, squinting into another sunny South Florida afternoon.

She halted in her steps when she realized that the voice she heard talking on a phone in front of the restaurant came from Danielle herself. Covertly, Clara flashed a glance at her. Danielle was still pretty, but a slight redness in her face and circles beneath her eyes made her look more human than in her website photo.

Hovering politely near the ixora bushes Clara tried not to eavesdrop, but she'd already come too close and turning around would look even more awkward.

"No, no," Danielle was saying into the phone. "Don't—don't you—no. Don't you dare. If you — no, listen to me, Ashley. They don't *mean anything*. I'm so sorry they hurt you like that, but they're wrong. Listen — if I came up to you and told you your dog was made of carrots and shit ranch dressing, would you believe me just because I'm your teacher?"

Clara giggled, and tried to hide it because she was pretending not to listen. My, my, these little pink flowers were *fascinating*...

"I hear you giggling, Ashley. I want you to take that giggle and paint it for me. Then I want you to solemnly promise me *not to show it to them*. As far as I'm concerned, they've lost the right to teach you. People like that drive wonderful, talented little ducklings like you right out of the art world."

Danielle paced back and forth in front of the restaurant, fidgeting with a decoration on her purse that looked like a lime. Wait, was her whole purse an *avocado*? "Well, *I* don't care if all you want to draw is mermaids. Keep on drawing mermaids. Fuck, draw *me* as a mermaid. Give me a big ole anglerfish on a leash, too. No, not anglerfish. What are those... those terrifying one with the... with the teeth—"

Danielle's free hand flailed around as she dithered.

"Viperfish," Clara blurted out without realizing it.

Danielle spun around.

Clara, her face suddenly a campfire, could only hold up a knitting project and grin shamefully.

"Draw me as a mermaid with a viperfish on a leash. Diamond studded collar. And every time one of those *schmegegges* comes out with some more crap about representational art being less, imagine what those teeth can do. Because I promise, I take very good care of my pets' dental work... okay, you okay now, Ash? My lunch meeting is here. But don't you fucking dare destroy that painting. Promise me. Promise me. Okay. Good girl. See you Tuesday."

Danielle hung up the phone, slightly breathless. Compared to her glamorous website picture, with hair slightly out of place and face a little blotchy, she was less beautiful, but more arresting.

Danielle stuck out her right hand with all the force of a weapon, but with a grin that disarmed it. "Hi, I'm Danielle Solomon, and I fucking support representational art. How are you?"

"I'm Clara, and I have a mermaid poster in my bedroom!" Clara quipped. Well, okay, there were two mermaids in the picture and they were making out, but still.

"Don't worry; I wouldn't have canceled the yarn deal if you liked abstracts." Danielle waved one hand reassuringly as she used the other to hold the door open for Clara. "I just feel really strongly about letting people, you know, like what they like. And that's twelve times more important when you're talking about the actual artist, *making* the stuff. Two, please!"

"Booth or table?"

They ended up in a booth by the window, and put in their orders. "Thank you so much for coming out to meet with me," Clara gushed. "I've gotten really excited about this project, and I hope you like what I came up with."

"I don't know if I know enough about knitting to know if I like it or not," said Danielle, "but what I do know I like, is the idea of my paintings inspiring a whole yarn collection. I mean, who wouldn't!"

Clara shrugged. "A lot of people haven't realized how big knitting is. They still associate it with grandmothers and pregnancy."

"In other words, with desexualized women," Danielle pointed out. "And therefore, it becomes devalued."

"Hmm," said Clara, pondering. "I never made that connection before."

"Fair warning—I'm kind of a big obnoxious feminist."

"You don't seem obnoxious at all!" Clara chattered. "Those things you were telling that student on the phone sounded really encouraging. Not that I should have been listening, obviously. Sorry!"

"Hey, I'm the one who decided to have a big public conversation in the breezeway instead of in my car. Ooh! Pickles."

That would be the waitress coming back with small bowls filled with crispy half-sours and fluffy little onion rolls.

"I could just fill up on this stuff," Danielle said through her mouthful of bliss.

"I'm glad you like this place. I come here with my family all the time."

"Yeah, me too." A weird look that almost reminded Clara of a crack spreading across thin ice settled over Danielle's face.

She hastened to steer her away from whatever it was. "Our people really do have the best comfort food."

Danielle nodded slowly. "Chicken soup that takes the whole day to make."

"Bagels and lox with all the trimmings."

"Brisket."

"Noodle kugel, the kind with peaches and raisins."

"Gefilte fish?" Clara grinned mischievously.

"No, now I can't talk to you anymore," Danielle kidded.

Clara shrugged. "*I* like it."

"Good, you can have my share. Along with matzo."

"I'll pass!" Clara rifled through her portfolio, making sure the pages she'd printed were in the right order to go with her sketches.

"Nobody actually *likes* matzo. It's basically a cracker with dysthymia."

"Gentiles do," Clara pointed out as she arranged her papers across the table. "Ever complained to one of your Christian friends, or like, atheists who were raised Christian or whatever, during Passover? They always say they like it." And every once in a while she ran into someone Jewish who did, too, but that wasn't as common.

Danielle studied the pages in front of her, where a close-up of a coconut palm in the sun was paired with a variegated yarn in greens and yellowish-oranges that matched its tones. "Oh, wow, you really distilled this down to its color skeleton."

Clara beamed. "That's good, right?"

Danielle nodded. "It's like you were working from a picture of my original palette." She moved on to the next grouping of sketch with painting. "How does this work?"

Clara had transformed roseate spoonbills walking through the water at sunrise into a shimmery combination of pale blues and silvers, with pink flecks scattered throughout. "Spatter dyeing is really in right now," she explained. "I've had people tell me it makes knitting shawls with long expanses of garter stitch more interesting."

"See, I don't even know what garter stitch is."

"Matzo for knitters," Clara quipped. "Okay, not really. But it's just.... the same stitch over and over. Sometimes you need to do it to get from point A to point B between the interesting parts."

"We have stuff like that in art, too," said Danielle. "It can be meditative. Relaxing. Soothing. Or just frustrating, depending," she added. "Can I take a picture of some of those?"

Clara nodded. "I mean, like, none of this is finalized. These were just my initial ideas. I'd have to do a bunch of test skeins first, might even knit swatches..." Danielle had her phone out and was already happily snapping pictures. Now that Clara could see the back of the phone clearly, she noticed a familiar pawprint symbol. "Is that Captain Werewolf?"

Danielle nodded. "Yeah. I know—"

"No, I *love* that show! That's the only way I get through the most boring parts of knitting projects. Like a really long shawl border." Clara took another pickle from the dish. "Are you caught up?"

"No, I'm three episodes behind, but I got spoiled about the—wait, are *you* caught up?"

"Yeah, I'm good." Clara snickered. "I read fanfic so I'm paranoid about being spoiled by some thirteen year old's plot summary."

"I wish they'd just let Cinnamon Blade and Soledad be together in canon already."

Cinnamon Blade was the redhead whose hair Clara had been thinking about turning into a club colorway. "Me, too! I can't resist that bad girl - good girl vibe they've got going on." Little points of heat prickled in her face as she realized she might be talking to a lady who walked on her side of the rainbow.

Danielle shrugged. "At least we can console ourselves that as long as it's just subtext they can't kill them off like all those other shows."

"Yeah, true."

"Perfect get-rich-quick scheme—life insurance policies on all the lesbians on sci fi shows." Danielle pointed at Clara. "Am I right? I'm right. Foolproof."

Danielle took out a sketchbook and a pencil, but just then the waitress arrived heavily laden with goodies. "*I did that,*" she mock-bragged to Clara, pointing at the book as she pushed it aside.

Clara put away her printouts and sketches and dug in. For a few moments both women thought only of food, but eventually conversation revived. "So what kind of legal protections would you want for me to go through with this?"

"Well, I mean..." Danielle paused to take a long sip of her Dr. Brown's. "Nothing major. I mean, it's not like I have to tell you not to have homophobic ads or whatever."

Clara burst into self-conscious giggles. With flared jazz hands and a funny robotic voice, she said, "Don't buy my yarn—I am too gay." Her heart was beating in her face from how inane that sounded, but she was also glad for the opportunity to come out in the natural flow of conversation.

Danielle responded to this with a sort of contented cat-face, heavy-lidded and smiling subtly, as if Clara's admission relaxed her. "Speaking of, have you ever dyed any of the identity flags?"

"When I first got into dyeing I did the ace flag for a friend, but I didn't use enough mordant to fix the plum dye to the yarn and it bled into the white part. So it was, like, plum, silver, black, and *pink*. She liked it anyway, though."

"It sounds pretty," said Danielle.

"I was going to do bi colors next but that was the time I used too much dye and it was coming off on my hands when I tried to knit with it. Made me get sick of those colors *really* quickly."

"The bi colors look like shit." Danielle picked up the parsley garnish from her plate and stuffed it in her mouth. "I'm bi, by the way. If I could trade our flag with the ace one for a hundred dollars I'd take it."

"Is that the hundred dollars you got for taking out life insurance on the dead lesbians on TV?"

Danielle smirked at her and snapped her fingers.

"So, any *real* rules?"

"My dad's a lawyer. How about I get him to draw something up that we can sign that says anything you dye based on my paintings has to credit me and have my full name and website?"

"Yeah, that sounds fair," said Clara. "What about royalties?"

Danielle waved her hand. "Don't worry about it."

"Are you sure? I don't want to feel like I'm exploiting you—"

"If it goes well, you can take me to dinner."

Clara knew right then that she was making the face Jasmine would have recognized from Daniel Greenbaum's bar mitzvah.

The next week flew by as the box office kept Clara busy during the day and the dye-pots — in her case, gigantic kettles like the ones Italian grandmothers ladle spaghetti from in ads for pasta sauce — at night. She tested her ideas, hanging wet yarn up to dry in all the bathrooms until Jasmine protested and started leaving mocking post-it notes on the mirrors. "If I'm gonna live in a preschool," read one in her distinctive loopy handwriting, "can I have Playdough for dinner?"

Like any other week, she topped off her evening reading fanfiction on her laptop in bed. On Tuesday night, when she finished a particularly toothsome vignette about Soledad and Cinnamon Blade, she realized that maybe Danielle would like it too. It was short, so it wouldn't come with the pressure of "here, read this 75,000 word story!" Plus, it was G-rated, so she wasn't doing something as inappropriate as sending a sexy link to someone who was, at least for now, a work contact.

She shot over the email before she could chicken out. After she sent it, she realized she'd included more smilies than was probably normal.

Danielle must have read it late at night after Clara already passed out, because she woke up to a two word email — *omg, cute!*

That night when her next batch of test skeins were drip drying in front of the box fans she borrowed from the theater, she glanced at her email. Danielle had replied again—*Have you seen this one? It's longish but worth it.* Included was another fanfic link.

Clara showed her appreciation by sending her tiny reaction emails as she progressed through the chapters.

Thursday the email arrived with the papers Danielle's dad had prepared. "Can I swing by your work Friday morning and pick it up?"

"Sure," Clara emailed back. "I'm at the performing arts center box office. If I'm not at the window when you come, just ask for me."

She scanned the contract to make sure everything both women had agreed on was there. Good, they'd remembered the clause about Danielle not having veto power or any other kind of dramatic recourse if one of the colorways didn't knit up to her taste. Not that she expected the generous, encouraging woman to do that, but she'd seen enough drama in the yarn world to anticipate problems.

At least I'm not faking my own death to get out of sending people their yarn, she mulled with dry amusement. "Help, I am too dead to dye," she murmured out loud, pouting that Jasmine wasn't home to hear that incredible free-range organic pun. Pity.

She had bad luck with the fanfic browsing that night. One ran that risk when it was all free — not that published fiction wasn't its own kind of crapshoot — but she must have been clicking under a bad star. First she wasted time with one that went nowhere, and then *two in a row* wound up being racist. "I know it's free, but I would literally pay for a racism filter," she bellyached to Danielle in a quick email that made her feel better for having a place to send it.

When Danielle stepped up to the box office window on Friday morning, Clara had to remind herself to breathe. She looked like the website photo again—a princess from a forgotten time, the heroine of an opera, an artist's muse. *Is she my muse if my yarn colors come from her paintings, or does that make her my muse once-removed? Second muse? Muse-in-law?* "Hi," Clara stuttered out loud, smiling a lot. "You look really nice."

"Thanks—I'm dressed up for shul already," Danielle explained, waving one sleeve of her purple mock-Ren-fest blouse. "I hate laundry, and I don't teach today anyway so

I might as well." She slid a paper under the ticket window. "Here. Sign over your immortal soul, Faust."

Clara scanned the document briefly just so she wouldn't have to admit to her parents that she'd signed something without reading it first, but her mind was still skipping around like a preschooler on a sugar high. *Step-muse?*

"Oh, and I brought you this." Danielle passed another piece of paper through the tray.

It was a pencil drawing, hasty yet full of skill and motion. Captain Werewolf's sidekick Cinnamon Blade, a reformed cat burglar, had scaled the side of the office building where Soledad worked and was kissing her through an open window. "Holy shit," Clara exclaimed, unable to contain her sensation of her glowing heart.

"Did that last night after I got your email,"
Danielle explained, tossing a lock of her
long black hair out of her face. "You like it?
Does the trick?" Dark dancing eyes
scanned Clara's face.

"This is everything I ever wanted out of fan
art," Clara murmured.

"I'm glad." Danielle looked satisfied, and
leaned with both elbows on the box office
counter. As she peered through the
window at her handiwork, Clara got an
eyeful of miraculous cleavage.

"So, now that we've both signed this, I can
start posting about it, right?" Clara passed
the contract back through the window.

Danielle nodded. "I'm totally stoked. I
hope some of these people are local;
maybe we can get them to take pictures
with the stuff they make from the yarn,
next to the painting."

"That would be super cool!" Clara beamed.

An older couple walked up behind Danielle, and she moved away from the window so Clara could get back to work. "See you later!"

It was only after she'd helped the couple pick out their seats that she realized she didn't know if Danielle did, in fact, stay offline during Shabbat. She'd better post on Saturday night, then, just in case. So they could both be there to promote it.

Clara, high on the adrenaline of creativity, worked late into the night on Friday poking and prodding her online sales pitch. She took pictures of some of her sample yarn, arranged it with Danielle's paintings, and wrote and rewrote her ad copy until the word 'color' stopped making sense.

Even her breaks were productive, feverishly knitting a disconnected ankle for a sock that would never exist so she'd have a picture of at least one of the colorways knitted up. She cycled through a number of Captain Werewolf fan-made music videos before switching to a cooking competition.

She passed out some time around three in the morning and dreamt of Cinnamon Blade defeating villains with an eggbeater.

Saturday was still a work day for her this week, so Clara doubled up on coffee and did the best she could. Luckily, she was still pumped up from how excited she was to launch her second ever sock club.

Finally, the matinee performance was over; the evening crew came to relieve her, and she was on the road headed for home.

Just a few more touches needed and the page would be live!

After a quick dinner with Jasmine, she texted Danielle. *I'm ready to post. Are you good?*

I'm ready to signal boost! Best of luck :) Danielle replied.

Clara checked her handiwork one more time before calling to Jasmine, "Hey, can you count me down?"

"Cla-ra, Cla-ra, Cla-ra," Jasmine chanted, punching the air with every syllable like a Dolphins fan.

"Yay! Wait, that's not counting."

"I was in Base Clara."

"I'm in your base, killing your dudes," Clara retorted.

"Old meme is old."

Clara stuck out her tongue.

"*Fine*. Three, two, one, press the stupid button."

Clara dramatically clicked on her laptop. "And we have liftoff!"

Five minutes later, she'd tweeted, Facebooked, and probably most importantly, Raveled about it.

An email came in from Danielle. *Looks great! I love how much work you put into this. I have complete confidence. Gonna go signal boost now.*

"Are you refreshing Ravelry every twenty seconds?" Jasmine smirked as she leaned against the fridge.

"I'm not *not* refreshing Rav every twenty seconds." Clara grinned. Just then, her phone chirped. "Did I make a sale??"

"Did you make a sale?" Jasmine echoed.

"I made a sale!"

Clara and Jasmine jumped up and down together. "Okay, holy shit, I'm tired."

"How late were you up last night?" asked Jasmine.

"...Yes."

"Go to sleep."

"But the *thing*."

"Thing can thing in the morning." Jasmine started to lightly shove Clara by the shoulders out of the kitchen.

"But what if there's a problem? Like if the site goes down and—"

"And you need to be taking care of that while you're dead on your feet? They know you're just one woman in your kitchen, right?"

 "One woman and the world's greatest sister." The Phantom chose that moment to weave figure eights around both their ankles. "And her stupid tuxedo cat," Clara added.

Jasmine was right. Clara was asleep ten seconds after her head hit the pillow, and this time she didn't remember her dreams.

She woke up Sunday morning with beautiful sunlight streaming in her window and the heaviness of an adult male cat on her chest. The third and final component of a glorious morning was the remembrance that when she turned on her phone, she'd see sales. At least, she *hoped* she'd see sales!

...three hundred and five????

She put the phone down and took a moment. Was she still dreaming? Had she read it wrong? No, because "30.5" wouldn't make any sense. She hadn't set it up where anyone could *do* "half" the sock club. Wait, was that 305 like the Miami area code?

No. It was real. There were really that many notifications in the shopping cart app.

What the shit...?

Clara nearly crashed into Jasmine on her way into the bathroom. "Sorry, I..."

"You look confused. Toilet's that way. Close to the floor, looks like a really small bathtub."

"Very funny."

"What's going on?" Jasmine called from the other side of the bathroom door. "That's not your happy face. No sales?"

"...Oh, I had sales!" Clara replied from the toilet. "I had over three hundred sales!"

"What!?" Jasmine's squeal was ear-piercing. "That's amazing! I'm so happy for you!"

"Wait," Clara countered. "That's way more than I can handle. What do I do?"

"Who gives a shit? Doesn't this mean you have, like, five figures you didn't have yesterday?"

At this, Clara was stunned again. All she'd been thinking about was the extra work. Now visions of simple luxuries began to hatch from their shells —Turkish Delight with pistachios, that really nice set of interchangeable needles, maybe tickets to something on Actual Broadway.

"I might have to file quarterly taxes," she realized out loud.

"What happened?" Jasmine asked.

Clara emerged from the bathroom. "I don't know yet. I haven't checked Twitter or anything. Maybe someone told the Yarn Harlot or Franklin Habit."

"On the *first night* of the ad? I mean, yeah, I guess it's possible. Oh, by the way, we're meeting Mom and Dad and Zayde for linner."

"Okay. At their house?"

"Yeah. She's making salmon."

"That's *perfect*, because I already feel like I'm swimming upstream."

"Deep, man." Jasmine snapped her fingers with mock-beatnik sincerity, then left Clara to herself on the sofa.

Clara stared at her phone. She wanted to call Danielle, but she didn't want to sound disappointed about her terrifying good news.

She dialed the call before she chickened out.

"Hello?" Danielle's voice was husky— almost unnaturally so.

"Hey, good morning!"

"How are you?" Her voice cracked.

"Wait, sorry, did I wake you up?"

"No, I—no, you're fine. Excuse me one second?"

Clara waited patiently until the sound of rustling and sniffling had cleared. She hoped Danielle hadn't come down sick.

"Okay, I'm back. So how did we do?"

"Well, we kind of... broke the house. When I woke up, it was at three hundred and five sales."

"Wow, Clara, that's terrific!" Now Danielle's voice sounded like the sun had burned off the haze after a morning of bad weather. "Oh, that's so great. Such good news."

"Oh, it's terrific, but I'm scared to death!" Clara ran her fingers through her hair. "I only had twenty-five last time. I never thought I'd have more than fifty, maybe seventy-five. It didn't even occur to me to put a limit on signups. I never imagined—"

"I'm sorry," said Danielle. "I think this might be my fault, indirectly, anyway."

"What do you mean?"

"My uncle retweeted your post."

"Your uncle?"

"Snowplow Solomon," said Danielle. "The comedian?"

"*Snowplow Solomon is your uncle??*"

"You scared the cat!" Jasmine groused from another room.

"Snowplow Solomon as in, everybody's Meme Grandpa?" Clara was in shock.

"Yep, that's my Uncle Dave." Danielle seemed to be taking Clara's reaction in stride.

"Okay, no wonder my shopping cart is blowing up. Okay. Okay, I can do this. Okay."

"We've got this. Breathe." Danielle's voice was commanding, reassuring, a solid wall of feminine strength. "You can close sales now, right?"

"Yeah."

"Can you get more blank yarn?"

"Oh, I can get more yarn," Clara reassured her. "It's just about finding the time."

"Can I come over and help? Even if you have to paint the yarn yourself, I can help wrap packages."

"I would *love* your help." Clara's skin
tingled at the idea. "You can help wind."

"I kinda feel like I have to," said Danielle.
"Really, I didn't understand how small-
batch this was. But we'll make it work!"

"Snowplow freaking Solomon."

"Which one is Snowplow Solomon?" Mama
Ziegler spooned a second helping of green
beans that Clara hadn't asked for on to
Clara's plate.

"*College U?*" Clara's father tried helpfully.
"He was the friend. The one who winds up
with the supermodel. And he was the
uncle on Triplet Trouble."

"What's he doing these days?" asked Clara's mother.

"He's basically become an internet celebrity for being a wiseass and reposting funny pictures," said Jasmine. "Like, half the people who follow him are under twenty-five."

"Babies." Mama smiled indulgently. "Do they even know he was on TV?"

"Probably only from YouTube clips," said Clara. "And, like, reaction shots and stuff."

"He was also the swim instructor on..." Zayde paused for a moment. "*Resort Miami*. That was the name of the show! Bubby always enjoyed when he was on. She laughed and laughed..." Then he started quoting catchphrases.

"Oh, *that* was him?" said Mama. "I remember that show."

Clara didn't mean to tune them out, but they seemed happy enough discussing sixties television and her worries were starting to fill her skull like balloons inflating in a shoebox. What if she ran into supply problems? She'd better order all the yarn in advance just in case. And then stub her toe on the boxes every single night for the next year.

She couldn't even bear thinking about free time. This was a whole second job she'd just accidentally signed herself up for.

Clara suddenly realized that she'd eaten the last bite of her salmon, and she'd zoned the entire rest of the way through dinner. Daddy was clearing the dishes away, and Mama stood beside Zayde's wheelchair. "How do you feel, Pop? Take a couple of steps?"

"If the girls can walk me back to my chair, I think I can manage it."

Clara and Jasmine rushed to either side of him, each taking an arm. These arms had been so muscular in their childhood; Clara's heart quailed a little.

He settled into his armchair — His Armchair, Clara thought, always mentally capitalizing it — with a delighted sigh. "Now, if only I had my ice cream."

"I'll go get it!" Jasmine scampered off.

Zayde turned to Clara. "What's wrong? Dinner you were somewhere else."

Of course HE would be able to tell. Clara told him all about the sock club. "I am *so* in over my head," she concluded. "If I fu— mess this up, I'll get slammed all over the internet. And *not* messing it up means I

have way more work than I was
expecting."

Zayde smiled. "You can do it. You'll be
fine. You have help, right? Especially since
you got money up front?"

"Yeah, Jasmine's helping, and the artist
who gave me the idea for the colors."

"What about that Trina of yours?"

Clara flushed. "Trina and I broke up two
years ago."

"Oh, that's right. I knew that. Anybody
new out there? You know, I think the
Moskowitzes have a gay daughter... she
lives in Northhampton."

"I'm kind of interested in the artist lady,
actually," Clara admitted. "The one who's
Snowplow Solomon's niece."

"Snowplow Solomon! Your Bubby loved whenever he came on the screen! On *Resort Miami.* He was the swim instructor. His niece?"

"She's the reason I sold so much yarn." Clara explained again. Sometimes Zayde's memory problems could be a little bit of a funhouse ride, but she was used to it.

It turned out that Danielle was not, in fact, shomer Shabbos but only observant. "I go to temple every week, I fast on Yom Kippur, and I guess I keep kosher-lite or whatever," she explained over the phone. "Like, no pork, no shellfish, no cheeseburgers." Cheeseburgers aside, this meant she was free on Saturday afternoon to start helping Clara prepare and dye the yarn.

"Whoa!" she exclaimed as she passed through the door, taking off her sunglasses to stare at the boxes blockading the hallway.

"Yup," said Clara proudly. She felt deliciously official in her brand-new Captain Werewolf apron, impulse-bought from a fan site on Etsy. "It's a real place of business now."

"So this is what three hundred balls of yarn look like all packaged up?"

"More like two thousand," said Clara. "Since everyone paid up front, I was able to make the minimum for an opening order with a really cool wholesaler. This is all six installments, minus what I've already been working on. Also, they're not balled up already. I sell them like this — it's called a skein, or a hank." She held up her test sample. "It's one of your roseate spoonbills. You like?"

Danielle squished the multi-layered riot of pinks and hints of blue. "This is such a neat experience for me," she marveled. "Yeah, I really like this one! Really does the flat-nose flamingoes justice."

"Wait, what?"

"Oh, I was just being a dick to this guy. He wasn't from here, so I started making stuff up. I told him what they really were, eventually, but he believed me at first!"

Clara shook her head, grinning. "So what I could really use your help with is tying off these skeins." She lifted an off-white, undyed hank from an open box on the table. "The company ships them to me tied off too tightly to dye evenly. I need you to cut their tie and use this scrap yarn to tie a new, looser tie, maybe four per hank. This is how you undo them." She unwound the skein into a huge loop about a yard across.

"Be super careful because when they're like this, if they're not tied up, they'll basically explode if you look at them funny."

"That's almost a *that's-what-she-said*, but it doesn't quite... nah. Nope. Turpentine." Danielle motioned as if she were scrubbing away her own bad joke from a canvas. Then she sat down and got to work.

In the nearby kitchen, Clara stuck her gloved hands into a pair of oven mitts and lifted an aluminum tray of dye, water, and yarn out of the oven. She set it on the counter next to a line of similar trays to cool. "Thanks so much for coming to help me out. I really appreciate it."

"Nah, this is my idea of fun. I could use the distraction, and I love learning about new ways to make art."

"Sorry I didn't give you something more creative to do!"

"Oh, shoot, I don't care!" Danielle snipped and tied happily in her corner. "Sometimes it's nice to just follow the directions. I'm glad you're making all the color decisions and I have no responsibility here. Just... glide."

"Tie knots and look pretty," Clara retorted, adrenaline swelling in her chest for following through with an Actual Flirt.

"*So much pressure*," Danielle barked in a mock-pout. "Hey, are you making pickles in there, too?"

"That's the yarn. I had to soak them in vinegar to set the dye."

"I suppose I will somehow live... without a pickle..."

"There's probably still half a jar in the fridge from when my grandparents still lived here, whenever you want to take a break," said Clara.

"Oh, this was their house?" Snip, tie. Snip, tie.

"Yeah, but when my grandma died, my parents moved Zayde in with them because he's got, like, stuff going on and couldn't live alone. So my sister and I moved in."

"You guys get along?"

"Yeah, pretty much." Clara poured the water out of an already cool tray carefully down the drain, rinsing the skeins to make sure the water ran clear. "Much better than when we were kids. We were both pretty annoying. She was really into metal, and I kept blasting, like, Les Miz on full volume."

"Musicals seem to be moving in a direction that would make you both happy," Danielle observed. "More electric guitars and rock drums?"

"Yeah, I know what you mean. Whoops!" The Phantom wove in and out of Clara's legs, and she made sure not to do anything with pigment or large pans of water until he'd finished.

Then he trotted over to inspect Danielle. She held out her knuckles for him to sniff. "I'm guessing this isn't your sister shifted into a cat, right?"

Clara grinned. "That's The Phantom. Like Phantom of the Opera, because of the tuxedo coloring and white face."

"Oh, my God, that's *perfect*," Danielle gushed. "You should sneak him into a church and get a picture of him walking on the organ."

"Or swinging on a chandelier." Clara swung the skein she was holding as if to illustrate, sloshing water on the floor.

"And absolutely nobody will get us arrested for this."

"Well," Clara began boldly, "not if you *paint* it..."

Danielle snipped and tied, snipped and tied. "I haven't actually painted in a while."

"Oh, yeah?" Clara noted that the air felt a little heavy suddenly.

"Stuff."

Clara didn't know what to say, but she also knew not every silence had to be filled. Sometimes the white spots, those left undyed and natural, were integral to the beauty of a colorway.

"I did some more pencil studies of Cinnamon and Wolfie last night, but it was just more fandom garbage," Danielle continued.

A noise at the door heralded Jasmine's arrival. She threw her purse into the couch, calling, "Hello, new person."

"Danielle, this is my sister Jasmine," Clara called from the kitchen.

"Hey," said Danielle.

"What are we doing? Still tying loops?" Jasmine floated around the kitchen, only half seriously looking for snacks before finding a water bottle.

"If you can stand more of this and you're not too tired from work," said Clara.

Jasmine waved the idea away and sat down at the table. "Whatever. I'm not standing up or getting yelled at by tourists."

"Where do you work?" asked Danielle.

"OasisLand," said Jasmine. "Get this — today someone wanted to know if the animatronic dinosaurs were real."

Clara was speechless for a moment before exclaiming "Well, they're real robots!"

"Seriously, next time someone asks me that I'm going to tell them *I'm* not real." Jasmine guzzled water before joining Danielle in the land of snipping and tying.

Clara held up a mason jar. Unsurprisingly, given the subject of the painting, she was running low on one of the two different pinks she was using. Time to mix more.

She opened the jar marked "Flamingo Pink," smirking as it made her remember Danielle's quirky misnomer. It didn't look pink at all in powdered form — more brown. She reached for a measuring spoon, but at just that moment, she seized up and sneezed.

Straight into the jar.

An explosion of fine pigmented dust scattered across the room. "Shit!" Clara put the jar and the spoon down carefully and then stood frozen, her eyes screwed shut.

"What happened?" called Jasmine from the other room.

Clara heard footsteps and then Danielle's voice, nearby. "Where are your towels?"

"The scrap ones are over there." Clara pointed. Then she felt the soft slide of fur against her ankle. "Oh, my God! Grab the cat."

Danielle started to laugh. "Phantom, huh? More like Sweeney Todd."

Clara took the towel from Danielle and wiped off her face carefully, then opened her eyes. The Phantom was struggling in Danielle's clumsy grasp, much of his white fur streaked with brilliant reddish pink. "I need to wash his feet." She tried not to think about the mess on the floor or the countertops. "Otherwise he'll get it all over the house or lick it off or—"

"Shh, we're cool. We got this." Danielle carried the cat to the kitchen sink. He squirmed all the way like a basket of snakes. "Can you turn on the faucet?"

Clara did, but it took both of them and several towels to subdue the poor creature as they scrubbed the pink out of his little white socks. Naturally, he shook a lot in the process.

Jasmine showed up just as the fun was ending, to check things out. By this point, The Phantom's wriggling shenanigans had spread a fine mist of pink droplets over all the flat surfaces near the sink, including the backsplash. "Oh, wow, pinkmageddon."

"Pinktastrophe," Danielle added.

"The Pinkening," Clara piped up.

"At night, all cats are gray," said Danielle in a voice that sounded like a movie trailer announcer, "but by day, *the pink stands out*."

"I think if this had ever happened to the actual Phantom of the Opera I'd have liked the show better," Jasmine observed as she resumed her post at the table.

The cat himself licked the sink water from his fur indignantly, but at least it wasn't pink dye.

Clara exhaled deeply. "Okay. It's not on any of the yarn, so we're good. This is just... a thing that happened."

"An adventure!" said Danielle.

Clara's regular knit and crochet night was at one of the local LGBT centers every alternating Thursday. Sandwiched between a Tae Kwon Do studio and a pizzeria that had changed names three times since Clara was in high school, the center stood as a humble gathering place in tropical suburbia.

"Today in parasitology—" began Marisol, while freeing a strand of black hair that had formerly been hers from her knitting project.

"That's what the Marisol doll says when you press the button on the back of her neck," quipped Tae, her girlfriend.

"Hey, it's not my fault the damn class is so interesting!"

"I like your stories! You should, like, knit a tapeworm," said Aren, the nonbinary high-school kid. This week, their hair was hot pink, with an undercut. "Can't they get like fifty feet long?"

"Mmm," said Ritchie, in his best size queen voice with a smirk to match.

"Okay, *ew*," said Tae.

Clara sat comfortably in the old leather sofa, donated by somebody's estate, and just listened to the banter.

"If you stopped eating meat we wouldn't have to worry about any of this," pointed out Becca as she paused in her knitting to lay her hand on her pregnant belly for a moment. "Oof."

"Actually, that's not true—" Marisol began calmly, before being interrupted by a jangle at the door.

A willowy trans girl in cobalt blue hipster glasses was letting herself in while juggling Starbucks, her project bag, and a pair of inline skates. "Hey, everyone!"

"A Wild Lindsay Appears!" called Tae.

Clara waved from the sofa, and Lindsay plopped down next to her.

"Congratulations! How's the sock club going so far?"

"Well, I think I'm gonna be okay..." Clara grinned uneasily. "I mean, I'm not getting as much sleep as I should, but I've got a ton of the first month dyed already. Jasmine's helping. And Danielle. Hey, if any of you want to come over and help, I can pay."

"What about volunteer hours? For scholarships?" asked Aren hopefully.

"Um," said Clara. "Let me look at the guidelines for your scholarship and I'll find a way to make it work."

"Is this the first month?" Lindsay fondled the fingerless mitten growing from Clara's needles, and Clara nodded. "It's gorgeous! I'm so glad I got my spot right when you posted instead of putting it off."

"Thanks!"

"Yeah, it's really a knockout. People will be talking about that," Tae agreed.

"I hope they say mostly good things," said Clara. "I've already gotten some weird messages, like from someone who tried to get a spot the first night but her card was declined and when she got it fixed I'd already closed it. And a couple people in the club are asking for coordinating solids for *all* the heels and toes, not just when I feel like it, and that's not what my plan was."

"It's all about boundaries," said Marilyn, a fat, middle-aged trans woman wearing a flowing hippie skirt and a black teeshirt where the slogan "Ignorance = Fear, Silence = Death" was punctuated by Keith Haring art in white. "I've been selling these canes longer than some of you've been alive, and I could tell you some stories." She gestured with her own cane, which was handpainted to look like a rattlesnake. "Customer wants it 'more green, like a shark.' Customer wants me to sign a waiver that I'll never make another one exactly like it. Customer wants me to put a *goddamn blade* inside. How does that saying go? No is a complete sentence?"

Clara nodded. "You're totally right. I'm trying my best." Marilyn was the oldest one among them and could be counted on to have something wise to say whether the topic be queer liberation or a particularly thorny instruction in a knitting pattern.

"Give them an inch," said Marilyn gravely, thumping her cane on the ground, "and they'll take Broward Boulevard."

"And get stuck in traffic," Tae quipped.

"A Christmas shark could be green," said Ritchie.

Everybody looked at him, dumbfounded by the non-sequitur. Tae spoke for the room. "The fuck is a Christmas shark?"

"Maybe if it had algae growing on its scales," Marisol suggested helpfully. "Actually, there's a microscopic organism that produces chlorophyll *and* swims—it's called *Euglena*."

"Are any of your yarns going to be green?" asked Aren.

"I can't *tell*," Clara giggled. "That'll spoil the surprise! But if you really wanted to, you could cheat and look at Danielle's website."

"Who's Danielle?"

"Danielle Solomon, the artist whose paintings I based this round of club on," said Clara.

"I love her stuff," Lindsay gushed. "I'm so glad you found her gallery! She makes me want to go hiking. Like a beach hike."

"She's been drawing me fandom art, too," said Clara, getting out her phone. "Wanna see?"

The sketch of Cinnamon Blade had shown up in the early dark hours, so that it was the first thing Clara saw when she dismissed her alarm. Dressed in the black Captain Werewolf costume instead of her silver catsuit, Blade stood on a cliff overlooking the ocean with her red hair unfurled in the wind. Clara was magnetized by the expression on her face — it wasn't so much a frown as a look of resigned disappointment and deep, deep pain.

Despite this, the picture still bore an overall message of strength.

In Soviet Russia, insomnia can't sleep YOU was Danielle's only garbled caption.

"Whoa, that's intense," Lindsay breathed.

Aren scampered over to see. "Is that Cinnamon Blade? Is that if Captain Werewolf died?"

"Danielle said it was for an AU where he betrayed the team and she had to take over," Clara explained.

"Whoa," said Aren. "I don't really read stuff that dark."

"Me, either, but I still like the picture." Clara's stomach felt vaguely queasy at the idea of Captain Werewolf doing anything like that

"She has a lot of talent," said Marilyn, glancing at the picture as Aren passed her the phone.

"I am *ridiculously* lucky to be working with her," Clara agreed. "She's the reason I sold so many. I had no idea, but her uncle is Snowplow Solomon and he retweeted my ad while I was asleep."

Ritchie suddenly sat upright in his chair, shifting his bulk forward. "Wait, Snowplow Solomon's Danielle's uncle? As in David Solomon the comedian?"

"Yeah, that's why I'm working overtime. Triple overtime. Wait, what's wrong?"

Ritchie bit his lip and furrowed his brow. "She okay?"

It was the last thing Clara was expecting him to say. "Yeah? I think so? What are you talking about?"

Ritchie's glance flitted around the room as if he were looking to the others for cues.

"Um. I saw a thing on a Facebook trending."

"I wish I could turn that off," Marilyn grumbled.

"I'll show you later," said Aren.

Clara felt a little sick. "Did he die today or something?" she asked cautiously.

"No, no, nothing like that." Ritchie put up one hand. "You know what? It's none of my business. But—Danielle might could use some... support. Or something." He paused. "You can look it up if you want but there's no reason it needs to come from me."

Clara wanted to shrink into herself. Was Danielle ill? Like, *seriously* ill? Well, she'd do her best to be whatever that meant Danielle needed.

Sinking lower into the cushy sofa, Clara remembered Danielle's response to her reaction to the picture. *It helped me last night when I couldn't get to sleep.*

Couldn't get to sleep...

Clara wound yarn on autopilot, the swift beside her spinning in pink delirium. The burning in her arm muscle only partially distracted her from sentences that had become her constant inner dialogue — what was in the news about Danielle's uncle? If he hadn't died, why would Danielle need support?

And, more cogently, what would it mean if Clara peeked?

Well, it was obviously something a lot of other people knew, so maybe it wasn't that big of an evil to just simply find out. Clara picked up her phone and loaded Facebook, then closed the tab. No. This felt incredibly tacky. Friends didn't find out about friends' life crises from the *news*. It was only her business if Danielle wanted to make it her business.

She turned the handle on the skein-winder more vigorously, annoyed with herself for obsessing. But it was hard to think about anything else. Even when she put on the *Fun Home* soundtrack full blast, she found herself singing along by rote but not really paying attention.

It couldn't have been a breakup—she'd never seen a headline announcing the divorce of a celebrity's relative, only the celebrity themselves. Some kind of sickness made more sense, although she wasn't really sure why that would be newsworthy—unless Snowplow had posted an Awareness post about it. Like if

Danielle had Lyme Disease or something, and Snowplow wanted to bring attention to Lyme. Marilyn from the knit group had Lyme once. She seemed serene about it now, but whenever Clara went hiking with Lindsay, she insisted on them both checking each other for ticks with fierce scrutiny afterwards, fired up by Marilyn's frank stories of impaired short-term memory.

Clara pulled the skein off the skein winder and twisted it into the fat, fluffy coil the customer would get in the mail.

Some kind of homophobic or misogynist rant coming from her uncle would definitely upset Danielle, but that would be out of the blue and completely inconsistent from Snowplow's usual ideology. For a brief moment she wondered if he'd suddenly announced he was converting to Christianity, but her intellect caught up with her imagination and she remembered that Ritchie wasn't the type of person to realize that someone like Danielle might find that distressing.

Was *Snowplow* sick? Or maybe Danielle's father, who was presumably his brother?

It couldn't be something innocuous like Snowplow outing Danielle without her permission, could it? Although maybe that wasn't as innocuous as Clara initially thought. Not everyone lived in Clara's happy liberal bubble. And it would explain Ritchie suddenly shutting himself up. Golden Rule, after all — never out anyone without their permission. That was an old one. It's not like Ritchie knew Danielle was out to Clara already.

At some point her brain entirely left reason and started coming up with things like *He's been called up for the House on Unamerican Activities Committee* or *It turned out he was an alien spy all along* — like the Disguisers on Captain Werewolf.

"This is dumb," she said to the cat, who looked back at her with big, blasé eyes. "Someone else is going to find out and tell me and then it won't even be my fault that I know without her wanting me to know." With a sigh, she picked up her phone again.

Hey, she texted. *One of my friends at knitting said I needed to send you some love and support but he wouldn't tell me why. I don't need to know why, but I want you to know you have my friendship and if you need me for anything, even if you just want to come over and break dishes in my back yard, I'm here for you.*

There. Feeling much better, she arranged the next skein on the swift, dragging the end over to the skein winder to begin rewinding.

Danielle texted back: *Thanks, Yarn Fairy. I really appreciate that. Looking forward to the next time I can help with club.*

I could use help winding the spoonbill colorway, Clara responded.

I don't teach tomorrow.

I'm off tomorrow, too! Want to come over after breakfast?

Danielle responded with a flurry of smiley faces and then a turtle.

As she lulled herself back into a trance of spinning pink yarn, Clara felt with satisfaction that it no longer mattered if Danielle told her what this was all about or not — she knew she'd done the right thing by not letting the accident of her uncle's celebrity take away Danielle's privacy, at least where the two of them were concerned.

Clara clicked OK on the print screen again, then stared at her printer while gnawing at her lip with increasing irritation. This was the fourth time she'd sent the Spoonbills at Sunrise yarn label to the printer, and the fourth time absolutely diddly-fuck had happened. The printer made a small coughing noise, like the cartridge had moved an inch, but nothing came out.

She checked the connection again, which was tight at both ends just as it had been two minutes ago. The knock at the door came just after she restarted her laptop — again.

Danielle stood in the doorway, a fashion plate straight out of the 1940's in her red retro halter-dress covered in white polka dots. She was even wearing winged eyeliner and red lipstick, and her black locks cascaded in casual waves over her shoulders. She held up a white paper bag. "Rugelach?"

Clara needed a moment to take this vision in. "Come on in. You look amazing!"

"Thanks." Danielle walked in and set the bag down on the table. She moved deliberately, cautiously, a little stiff, a little like she was on stage. The eyeliner was too perfect; the fashion plate, plates of armor.

"I was just printing some labels, or trying to." Clara fiddled with the laptop again, hoping her house was cozy and safe and distracting. "See? I keep sending it to the printer but it doesn't print. I guess it'll only cut into my profit a little if I have to go to the copy shop; it's more about the annoyance of adding another step that I can't just do between yarn stuff."

"Can I see?"

Clara pushed the laptop over.

Danielle clicked and dragged and clicked again. Clara noticed the hands working on her keyboard had bright red nails to match the rest of the ensemble. "There."

The printer chugged into motion, sucked in a sheet of heavy bond paper, and dragged its cartridge back and forth. "Wow, thanks! What happened?"

Danielle pushed the computer back to her. "It was trying to send the job to another printer."

"That's the only printer in the house," said Clara, her brow furrowed.

"It says," and then Danielle read off a string of of numbers and letters, ending with "and then another hyphen and TennisMama."

"That's at my parents' house." Clara rolled her eyes. "Oh, my God. It's not actually printing over there five times, right? I'd have to be on her internet?"

"Probably not," said Danielle, "but there *is* a way you can print to other people's printers if you're not there. I think you have to have a password, though."

"Wasn't there a case recently of someone sending anti-Semitic fliers to print out at college campuses?" Clara had woken up that morning with another thought— maybe Danielle's mystery trauma was something like that. Living in South Florida, Clara sometimes had the luxury of forgetting about neo-Nazis until the internet brought her back to reality.

"I think they were hackers," said Danielle, collecting her thick waves of hair in her hands and arranging them over one shoulder. She picked up a hank of Roseate Spoonbill yarn from the table and made a mock lasso with it. "So what are we wrangling today, cowgirl?"

Clara showed her how to use the umbrella swift and the skein winder, so that the already-dried pink loops of yarn could be reskeined into their final saleable form, and Danielle got to work right away.

"Man, my right arm's getting so much exercise!" she exclaimed as she pumped the crank. "I'm gonna come out of this looking like a fiddler crab."

Clara finished cutting labels once the printer finished with them, then retreated into the kitchen to mix more dye. She was *incredibly* careful not to sneeze over any open jars this time!

"Are you making more of the pink?"

"No, this is the mahi mahi one," Clara replied, stirring the water in the jar. She set it down and dove for a pile of yarn in the corner of the sofa, then tossed her quarry to Danielle. "Here."

Danielle looked it over beneath one admiringly arched eyebrow. "I'd totally wear this." It was electric blue with accents of yellow and green, like the fish.

"I can make you something with it." Clara checked the color saturation against her test swatch, then carefully added another quarter teaspoon of dye to the hot jar, stirring it until it finally dissolved.

"That'd be awesome! Like what?"

"I mean, there's always socks, but it's too hot down here most of the year to wear wool socks," Clara pointed out. "But a lacy scarf might be easier to deal with. Here, this is Jasmine's. I made it in a mystery knit-a-long and she fell in love with the way it turned out so I let her keep it."

Danielle held the filmy plum gossamer up to the light. "I was right to call you the Yarn Fairy. This is like something out of a fairy-tale. What's a mystery knit-a-long?"

"Remember how the colors in a sock club are a surprise?" said Clara. "This is like that, only for patterns. They tell you how much yarn you need at the beginning so you know how much to buy, and then only reveal a little bit of the lace chart at a time."

"She must be a pretty good sister to deserve something like this." Danielle held it to her chest with both hands and looked pensively into space.

"Oh, she's great. Now that we're both adults. Look, she made me a quilt for my birthday—she doesn't knit, she sews." Clara dashed into her bedroom and came out shaking the cat hairs out of the 'old timey Broadway'-themed quilt. She held it up for Danielle proudly. "I think she had enough fun treasure-hunting for all the weird fabric as I do sleeping under it!"

Danielle's response was not at all what Clara had expected. She was standing in place as if frozen there, trembling slightly, her eyes closed and her fingertips resting on the table. Sure enough, between the lids of those closed eyes escaped a couple of fat tears that rolled in a mascara-tinted streak down her cheeks.

Clara threw the quilt over the back of the sofa and approached her. "I'm here," she said gently.

"I'm my own art today," Danielle began quietly. "I got up and I wanted to feel good, so I put on the dress, and the beads, and the heels, and the makeup—like I'm my own canvas. And I just kept going. If I did my face, maybe I wouldn't cry. I haven't been able to paint in months, Clara." Danielle's eyes popped open, tears streaming out.

Clara handed her a tissue. Danielle took it and dabbed at the sides of her eyes gingerly, but used it mostly to ball into a wad in her stressed-out hands.

"I'm in so much pain. My brother—" Danielle sighed like a wind before a thunderstorm. "He was my best friend. He's always been my best friend. We laugh at each other's stupid jokes. We were there for each other. I can't." She stopped again.

Clara just waited.

"*He stole my identity*," Danielle began again in a more deliberate, louder, angry tone. "My credit is fucked, my life savings are down to — never mind."

"Oh, my God," Clara breathed. "I'm so sorry."

"He kept getting suckered into real estate deals that were each supposed to be 'Ooh, this is gonna make me a millionaire' or whatever." She pierced the air with scarequote fingers. "Except somehow it never worked out that way, and he blew through his own money and then things got weird, and *fuck*, and *fucking fuck*."

"I'm so, so sorry."

"This fucking sucks," Danielle spewed. "For weeks I've been wanting to ask you out but I haven't because this is who I am right now and you don't deserve all this anger and pain."

"Oh, my gosh, you ridiculous person." Clara took both her hands in hers. "I know you feel like that inside but that's not how it comes out on the outside."

Danielle looked at her through tear-streaked eyelashes. "Are you willing to hang out and do stuff even if I don't smile the whole time except if we see a dog on a skateboard or something?"

"Yes!" Clara nodded enthusiastically.

Danielle squeezed her hands, and Clara knew that was what Danielle felt like doing instead of smiling. "I'm so glad we met."

"Me too. But I'm sorry about what you're going through."

"I feel like I've lost my whole life," said Danielle. "All our childhood memories together, our *adult* memories... so much of the way I'd spend my life had him in it. Now, I feel like I've been put against my will on an alien planet called New Reality, and I can't get back home. Maybe home never existed, maybe home's destroyed. I don't know."

She started to sob for real, and instinctively, Clara folded her head down against her shoulder and held her. Warm tears soaked into Clara's apron and against her collarbone, and she inhaled the clean gardenia scent of Danielle's hair for the first time.

"Thanks," Danielle murmured, her lips feeling startlingly intimate against Clara's skin. "Anyway, he got arrested last week,

and the news found out because of my
uncle being a TV star."

"This must be so hard for your family."

"They're dealing with it. I was the one he
was closest with. Or so I thought. I don't
know." Danielle picked herself up again
and wiped a sniffly nose. "He stole from
Mom, too."

"Oh, gosh." Clara rummaged in a kitchen
drawer and emerged with a chocolate bar.
"I know this is only a drop in the bucket,
but will it help at all?"

Danielle half-smiled and held up her hand
in polite refusal. "Thanks, though."

"Wait, no, I know." Clara flung open the
refrigerator. "Pickle?"

Now Danielle was cry-laughing as she took the half-sour from Clara. "And I thought it was just the dye smell again!"

"So, I have no life right now, but if I can crank out enough of this yarn on schedule, you want to spend Sunday downtown with me doing random staycation shit?"

"Please," said Danielle. "I'm starting from scratch. I'd love to make some new memories."

"Have you really not been able to paint?"

Danielle shook her head.

"That sucks."

"Tell me about it," said Danielle. "It's like, oh, wow, my biggest form of self-expression and healing, and I can't use it to express myself and heal! Fantastic. It's hard to just *be* because if I sit there *being* I start *brooding*, and without 'be time' the paintings don't have any fuel." She sighed. "I want to go back to helping you wind yarn but I could use some winding down myself. Can you show me more pretty things? Crafts are art and art will make me feel better." She walked over to the quilt. "This quilt is amazing, by the way."

"Yeah, totally!" said Clara. "Ooh, I know. I never showed you the stuff I made from the first sock club."

Danielle perched on the sofa and waited as Clara went to her bedroom and fetched her finished objects.

"So, this is what the socks end up looking like." Clara passed them over. She was proud of the way the simple pattern she'd chosen showed off their varying intensities of rusty reddish-orange. "This is sort of... a lace *snood*, I guess? And this one's a shawl."

Danielle studied each one with both eyes and hands. "So soft." Her glance lingered over the shawl, a rich tapestry of silver-toned greens and blues with just a hint of pink. "Thank you for sharing all this with me."

"Should I put some music on while we work?" Clara suggested.

"Something loud," Danielle agreed.

Clara sat perched on a low brick wall beside the Intercoastal, working on her knitting project as she waited for Danielle. A bright sun beamed overhead, and the early afternoon was punctuated by the sounds of cutlery clinking and murmurs of brunch conversation in nearby restaurants.

She heard footsteps drawing close from the right, and turned to see Danielle walking up the path of tribute bricks in a strappy white sundress. "Hi, I'm looking for my date—have you seen her?"

"Dates?" Clara pointed up at the date palm above her head, feeling the heat crank up in her face behind her mischievous smile. Oh, that one was *awful*.

Danielle narrowed her eyes. "I may just let you live."

Clara stuffed the unfinished sock back into her purse. "You look really cute!"

"You, too!"

"Thanks!" Clara was wearing a little dress Jasmine made her out of cartoon sheep fabric. She stopped herself saying so — maybe she'd tell Danielle later but she didn't want to remind her of what she'd lost. She hopped off the brick wall. "Have you ever been on the boat tour?"

Danielle shook her head. "Not from here. But I'm up for anything!"

"Mostly it's just rich people's homes," Clara explained as they walked, "but there's usually a lot of gorgeous architecture and landscaping, and a few minutes of open water."

"Ought to be fun!"

They bought their tickets, and then Clara looked at her watch. "So, we've got a couple of hours. How do you feel about going across the street to the science museum? I know there's not much time, but I have a family pass so we can go in and out whenever."

The light was green, but there was a momentary break in cars so they scuttled across to the huge breezeway at the museum's entrance.

Once inside, they drifted over to the wildlife exhibits. Clara peered into the touch tank, watching the hermit crabs crawl in gentle underwater slow-mo across the pebbled surface. Danielle drew one finger across the shell of a living conch, her movements artlessly sensual.

"It likes you because it knows you won't eat its friends." Clara flashed her an impish grin.

"Look at this magnificence shape," Danielle almost purred in response. "That spiral comes from inside itself, without having to think about it at all."

More aquariums led into a cave, where they confronted a large tank containing—

"*Jew*fish?" Danielle wrinkled her nose. "It's the 21st century. Why?"

Clara cocked her head to one side. "Yeah, I've got nothing." The creature was as large as she was, dull and covered with spots.

"I wouldn't mind it so much if it looked like *that*." Danielle pointed at the lionfish in the next tank, beautiful and striped.

Another area housed the museum's snakes. One of them was in the process of shedding its skin, and Danielle pressed her face so close to the case to see that one of the volunteers gently asked her to step back.

"Hey, would you be weirded out if I sketched this real quick?" Danielle looked at Clara with wide, insistent eyes.

"No, I think that's awesome!" Clara sat down next to the gopher tortoise tank and took out her knitting. While Danielle took out her sketchpad and did studies of the corn snake, Clara watched the little ancient-looking beast lugubriously eat his lettuce.

"I feel you, Snake Friend," Danielle remarked to her subject when she was halfway through. "That's what *I* need, too."

Since Danielle had brought it up first, Clara felt safer asking. "How's your planet?"

Danielle smiled on only one side. "Still spinning!" She was silent for a moment, staring at the snake. "Half of it's all torn up and gutted, bombed-out… that's the bit I try to stay out of. Inside jokes from the back of the car on Disney trips when we were kids, the time we snuck out of the house in the middle of the night to see what school looked like in the dark… Like, that part of the planet's not even round anymore. It's been ripped out. But I'm getting pretty used to the safe half. I picture myself walking around, exploring it, looking for treasure. And every time I find something shiny, I take it with me, or I know where it is for later."

"Am I one of the moon rocks?"

"Martian Princess seeks Nice Jewish Girl for..." Danielle looked at the snake, as if was about to whisper her a suggestion for the rest of her flirty line.

"Distraction and cuddles?" Clara suggested brightly.

"Those are our initials," Danielle pointed out. "Maybe they can be our burlesque names."

"This dress isn't coming off in public!" Clara stuck out her tongue.

"I'm sure the Jewfish wouldn't mind if we went back in that cave—"

"They need to change that name."

"Either that or put me in there in one of those mermaid suits from Weeki Wachee Springs." Danielle struck a pose that somehow seemed mermaidlike. "A *real* Jewfish."

"Ohhh, you'd make such a good mermaid."

"I could be part of the mangrove exhibit." Danielle leaned back dramatically against the tree roots emerging like houses on stilts from the tanks. "I could be dangerous, though. I eat visitors."

"Wait a second, how is *that* kosher?" Clara teased.

"*You* look kosher," Danielle teased.

"I purposely didn't eat any bacon since Thursday, in case you wanted to kiss me."

"In *case*?"

Clara grinned sheepishly. "You've been going through stuff! I didn't want to push."

"I appreciate that." Danielle led her away from the wildlife exhibit and towards the escalator. "I think feeling good is important, though."

On the second floor of the museum was an area devoted to space exploration. The first thing Clara saw was a scale. "Oh, cool! It's set to the gravity of all the other planets." With the push of a red button, whoever stood on it could toggle through their weight on Mars, the moon, or somewhere even farther.

"I don't do scales," said Danielle confidently. "Scales just fuck us up. But if you're willing to squeeze up there *with* me, the numbers won't mean as much."

"And we don't have to press Earth," Clara pointed out.

"I'm glad you understand." Danielle exhaled. "On three?"

They held hands and then balanced precariously on the silver surface. "We're on the moon!" Clara yelped, heat flowing through her tingling skin at the close contact with Danielle's body.

She almost lost her balance and fell off the scale, but Danielle put an arm around her to steady her. "Hey," Danielle murmured.

"Howdy," Clara responded, nervous and blushing. "So which one of these is your planet?"

"Lemme show you how we kiss on Mars," said Danielle.

Her heart pounding, Clara drew near to her mermaid Martian princess and gave her the sweetest, most satisfying kiss one could manage in four seconds.

It wasn't much, but she came away with her lips wet and her body tingling for more. *Well, fuck, now I want to drag her into the bathroom and we have boat tickets*, Clara thought as she stood there dazed from desire.

Then she almost fell off the scale again, and they both hopped off of it laughing.

Clara laced her fingers into Danielle's hand, which strangely gave some relief to the longing that now stained her with brilliant pinks. "Oh, hey, it's probably boat time."

"Let's go stare at rich people's houses!"

Clara squinted into the sunlight to peer at the next house, a gorgeous little palace with its Spanish-inspired roof of red curved tile and fountain flanked by centaurs. The garden was a riot of coconut palms and bird-of-paradise plants.

"This one belongs to one of our own local philanthropists, Greg Johnson," said the tour guide's voice on the loudspeaker.

"I walk by that name on a plaque every time I go to work," Clara observed. "I'm sure you've heard this line before but ticket sales cover less than half of the cost of blah blah."

Danielle nodded. "I think one of my paintings is in that house."

"*What*? That's awesome! Which one?"

"It was a study of some sea grape foliage," said Danielle. "He bid on it at a charity auction. I got some of the money and the rest went to ALS research."

"That's really cool!" Clara exclaimed. "Do you still have a picture of it?"

"Yeah, except not on this phone. But actually, there's something else I wanted to show you."

Danielle rummaged in her purse and thumbed through a few screens before passing the phone over.

Clara shielded the phone from the unimpeded sunlight to see more clearly. An unfinished painting of greenish silver succulent plants of the type that look like roses stared back at her. "What's this? Wait — are you painting again?"

Danielle's face answered the question for her before she even spoke. "I'm painting again."

Clara beamed. "I'm so happy for you!"

"That's not the whole story. Look closer."

"I kind of can't — the sun's too bright."

"It's based on your yarn. From your first club."

Clara's lips parted slightly with emotion as she felt the divine symmetry of the moment wash over her. "Oh, my God; really?"

Danielle nodded. "I have more ideas, too. The one with the two or three different rusts? That's going to be a still life with a plate of lobster."

"You're okay painting food you don't eat?"

"You think about the way I eat more than I do," Danielle pointed out.

"I'm sorry." Clara licked her lips. "I guess I'm a little self-conscious since you're more observant than I am."

"I'm not even remotely judging you, trust me," Danielle reassured her. "I'm totally just a random human. Like, my bra has a hole in it."

"Where?" Clara couldn't help but ask.

"You'll find out later!"

"This next house," the voice from the loudspeaker continued, "was originally built by Valentina Cooper. She liked to say she was the winner of two Oscars — Best Actress for *My Immortal* and her husband, Oscar Hess."

"That's an amazing line," said Clara. "Remind me to remember it for Jasmine. Oh." She caught herself.

"You're allowed to talk about your sister," said Danielle.

"Okay, good," said Clara. "She made me this dress, by the way!"

"Really? It's terrific! I should have known they don't sell sheep dresses at the mall."

"Sorry if I was too, like, overprotective or whatever."

"It's fine, because I'm glad you care," Danielle pointed out. She gazed out over the open water as the homes of luxury rolled on past, and Clara watched her pensive face. "I need space to mope sometimes, though."

"That's totally normal," said Clara.

"If I'm stuck on my planet," Danielle pointed out, "I'm gonna plant flowers there."

Clara traced a flower onto the back of Danielle's hand and looked for yarn colors in the tropical estates ahead.

END

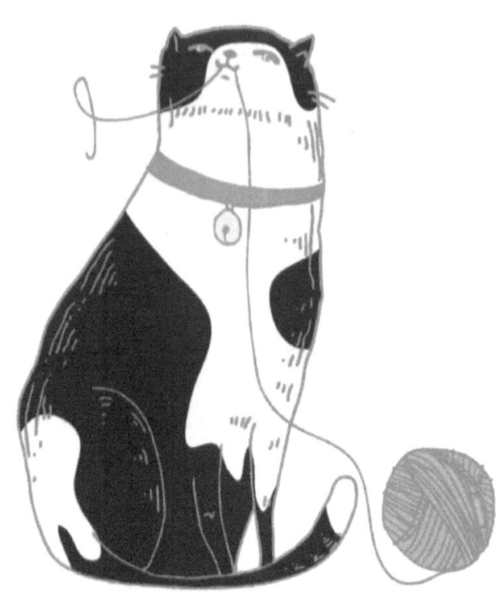

Note: Cinnamon Blade: Knife in Shining Armor, available in eBook, is a high-heat superhero f/f centering Cinnamon Blade and Soledad Castillo from Clara and Danielle's favorite fandom!

Fearless

Thanks for being at all my
All-State rehearsals, Mom,
and for constantly exposing me to
both classical music and
fiddle tunes throughout my life.

Fearless

♫

Robin's clarinet solo was startlingly beautiful as it drizzled through the hotel ballroom like maple syrup on pancakes. Anyone who had a few bars rest or whole notes turned to look at the skinny brunette—the other teens were clearly impressed. Even the Ricardo Montalbán look-alike conductor lifted his eyebrow to her and smiled.

From the glow on her face, Robin knew she'd knocked it out of the park. When the flute finally took the melody from her, she collapsed back into the folding chair and beamed toward the far side of the room.

Lana swelled with pride and gave her daughter a double thumbs-up in response, then held up her phone to mean *I got it on video!* A few more keystrokes and it was up on Facebook—*At All-State orchestra rehearsal, check out Robin's solo! So proud of my amazing kid.*

She was *damn* good. The rest of these kids were good too, of course—the best in the state. The last time Lana had played her violin was the mid-'90s, but she still had an ear for pitch, and it was a pleasure to be around high schoolers who knew where the notes were.

Robin and her friends had more solos coming up, so Lana flung her phone back into her purse and sat back to listen. Hey, the oboe player was pretty good, too!

The conductor stopped the group with a swipe of his left hand. "This is very good, I just would like a little more, *look* at me, so I can play with tempo, okay? Yaaa daaa da daaaa daaaa *daaaaa*..."

He let them finish the movement before calling a ten-minute break. Robin was ensconced in the middle of her band friends, talking animatedly, so Lana took her phone back out to check if anyone had said anything nice about the video yet. She wanted the whole world to be as dazzled by her kid as she was.

"Hey, you're Robin Novak's mother, right?"

Lana looked up and saw a familiar-looking woman wearing flannel and well-fitting jeans. She was a youthful fortyish with cropped black hair and heavy-rimmed glasses, and she was smiling invitingly.

Lana, out of the closet less than a year, fumbled the phone so hard that it flipped like a gymnast before landing on the floor between them. "Shit," she giggled, feeling fifteen instead of forty-three. Sure, there were plenty of straight women with short hair, but she was fairly sure this wasn't one of them.

The woman bent down to pick up Lana's phone just as Lana did, and their hands brushed. "It's not broken, is it?"

"Nah, these rubber cases… Yes, I'm Robin's mom; I'm Lana. I'm sorry, you look familiar but I can't…?"

"Melanie Feinberg," said the woman. "Call me Mel. I conduct the string orchestra and chorus at Tulip Tree High."

"Oh! Okay, yeah."

"She's really got it," said Mel. "Rafael said she's looking at going professional, right?" Rafael Vargas was the band director at Tulip Tree, and Robin's favorite teacher.

"Yeah, we've got audition trips planned for Julliard, Eastman, and Curtis," said Lana.

"I just can't get over that mature tone," Mel continued. "But, of course, all these kids are great. That's how they got into the top group."

"You have students here, too, right?"

"Yup!" Mel's face crinkled into a big grin as she pointed to two kids Lana recognized from the violin section. "They're mine, and so's the assistant principal cellist."

"That's great! Congratulations!"

"I also have a violinist and a violist in the ninth- and tenth-grade group," said Mel proudly. "We had a good year."

"I'm really enjoying these rehearsals," said Lana. "It's so nice to be around violins again. I go to all Robin's concerts, but the way they split up band and orchestra in the public schools mean I miss out on the entire string section." She ran her hand through her limp but abundant chestnut brown hair. "I used to play violin."

"What happened?"

Lana shrugged. "Job... kids..."

"Oh, you have other kids?"

Lana picked up her phone, taking care not to do any more circus tricks with it since she was still a little giggly and nervous around Mel. She showed her the home screen with Robin and Nick wearing reindeer antlers on their heads hugging in front of the Christmas tree. "He's at his dad's place while I'm here."

"That picture is *adorable*," said Mel. "Wow. Isn't that basically everybody's dream Christmas card?"

"Right? I could sell it and put all the money toward Robin's college."

"They should offer her real money, though."

"You think?"

"Okay, okay!" Maestro Lopez clapped his hands, ready to begin the rehearsal again.

Lana settled back into her seat, flushed and over-aware of herself. "Hey," Mel whispered with a hand on her shoulder. "I'm going to go over to the junior orchestra. Nice to finally talk to you!"

"Mm-hmm!" Lana smiled and watched her go.

Okay, now what?

Not for the first time, she felt a pang of resentful anger at the conservative culture in which she'd been raised, for leaving her no better prepared to flirt with women than a teenager was. When she and Steve got married, they "knew" they were doing the Right Thing, except it turned out it was all kinds of the Wrong Thing. Decades later, carried on the waves of the burgeoning gay rights movement they managed to free themselves, but now what?

Steve seemed to be getting along just fine. He was a lawyer and he already had a nice little clique of gay lawyers and realtors and a couple of small business owners. Meanwhile, Lana didn't even know where to start.

In the beginning, she thought she did, but cycling through memories of the past few months proved otherwise.

The lesbian meetups at the indie coffee house—sure, there was relief at not being the only one in the room, but she didn't really have anything else in common with the women who showed up.

The book club seemed like a great idea until she got too swamped with band mom stuff to read on time and chickened out of going back.

And the political group, campaigning for equal rights legislation, was really fulfilling because it was much easier to get to know strangers if you had a prearranged topic of conversation, but it turned out to be a great place to make friends with couples, widows, and energetic youngsters barely older than Robin. Not a potential girlfriend.

Fortunately, a dead Italian composer named Ottorino Respighi was all too ready to shake her out of her fretting. As the orchestra grew louder and the sound of the brass engulfed the room, she imagined the Roman army he'd been trying to evoke stomping on her worries as they marched.

♫

"Okay, we start with the Debussy when we get back here tonight! Have a good dinner!"

The conductor dismissed the eleventh- and twelfth-grade orchestra, and Lana was soon tackled by a hug 'round the waist. "This is so fun!" Robin exclaimed. "Everyone's so *good*."

"Did your friends have any plans for dinner? I can take everyone to Steak and Shake if you want."

"I dunno yet," said Robin, looking around and taking out her phone. "Lemme see if Blanca's group is done yet."

"What about Alexis?"

"She's still..." Robin drew closer and continued in the tiniest voice possible. "She's trying to get Tyler to invite her."

Lana grinned, spying Robin's friend talking to the second chair cello that Mel had bragged about. "Want me to play matchmaker? Go over there and invite them both."

Robin's eyes widened. "That's… almost brilliant."

"I'll wait for you out in the hallway." Lana gathered her things and pushed open the door to leave the ballroom.

She knew there would be a crowd of young musicians, parents, and teachers milling around, but she hadn't expected the air of alarm and confusion. The hotel staff were deep in discussion with furrowed brows, and some of the kids were just sitting in the middle of the floor surrounded by instrument cases and folders, looking lost.

Lana waved at Mel, who was standing by the free popcorn dispenser in the midst of a small flock of students. "Hey, what's going on?"

"The roads got snowed in during rehearsal," Mel explained.

"Greeeeat." Lana made a face.

"So I guess our choices are: lobby restaurant, or lobby restaurant." Mel smirked. "And then, of course, there's lobby restaurant."

"Don't forget the free popcorn!" said Lana.

"Nah, that's for the percussion section."

Robin emerged from the ballroom with Alexis and Tyler close behind. "Chicken fingeeeeeeers," she moaned in a zombie voice, her hands out in front of her still holding her clarinet case and folder.

"Change of plans," said Lana. "We're snowed in."

"You guys are totally welcome to join us in the hotel restaurant," said Mel.

"Anything, as long as it's made of food," Robin moaned. "Oh, and we have to wait for Blanca and her mom."

"Blanca Martinez? Flute?" Mel asked.

"Yeah, she's like, practically my sister," said Robin. "She got piccolo in the concert band this year. And she and her mom are rooming with us."

"Rooming with the piccolo player," said Mel, "that'll wake you up in the morning."

As soon as Blanca and her mom materialized from another ballroom, the three women led the group of teenagers over to the lobby restaurant. Naturally, by this point, there was a line, but the restaurant did its best to seat everybody—even if they were shoved off in a corner near the bathroom.

"Can you believe this weather?" said Mrs. Martinez after they gave the server their drink orders.

"Makes me glad we're stuck in here all day for three days anyway," said Robin. "It's all cozy."

"What about the concert?" asked Blanca. "Isn't that in the convention center?"

"They're connected," said Robin. "There's, like, a thing. Like a connecty-thing. You didn't see it last year?"

"The weather wasn't this fucked up last year," Tyler pointed out. "Oh, shit, I didn't mean to curse, Ms. Feinberg."

Robin burst out laughing. "Did you even hear what you just said?"

Lana couldn't help smile herself, and Mel definitely didn't seem to care about the language.

"You know what, though?" Mel pointed out, frowning. "The middle schoolers are out in that Holiday Inn three miles down the road. They're the ones who'll be in real trouble if they can't clear the snow."

"Oh, my God…" said Blanca. "I would *die*. I literally had nightmares I'd oversleep and miss getting here on time this morning."

"Then she practiced in Lana's van," said Mrs. Martinez.

"Oh, boy," smirked Mel.

Mrs. Martinez grinned. "They don't tell you when your daughter picks up the flute it comes with that shrill little torture device!"

"How does everybody like playing *Pines of Rome*?" Mel asked the students.

"Whales!" squealed Alexis.

"It's the whales from *Fantasia*!" said Blanca at the same time.

"I love the part at the end where the whales fly," said Robin, making flying-whale motions with her arms.

Mel met Lana's glance with amused eyes. "Before Disney did all that, it was supposed to be about different places in Rome," Mel explained. "When I hear you guys playing I think about my trips there. It's an amazing place, with thousands of years of history, art, culture—all overlapping. You could be standing between a building that's two hundred years old and columns that used to be part of another building that's two *thousand*."

"So romantic!" Blanca's eyes sparkled.

"Oh, man, that sounds awesome!" said Robin. "That's so cool that you've been there! The only part of Europe I've been in is Serbia, where my grandparents came from."

"Serbia has some Roman ruins, too," Lana pointed out. "There are some near Kladovo."

"Yeah, you don't have to go to Rome to see Roman ruins," Mel agreed. "Most of Europe has the odd column here and there. There's an incredible aqueduct about an hour outside Madrid. In fact, some of the sites in a city called Nîmes in Provence—France—looked just like some of the most amazing parts of Rome. A bridge, a temple, an amphitheater like the Coliseum…"

An image of Mel showing her around Europe's ancient wonders flipped into Lana's mind, and she smiled without meaning to.

Drinks came, followed by food, and Robin finally got her precious chicken fingers. Lana dug into her club sandwich, trying to balance her hunger with her intense wish to look graceful in front of Mel. Luckily, despite her heightened awareness, she didn't get mayonnaise on her nose.

Mrs. Martinez's phone chimed, and she chuckled when she looked at it. "Oh, boys. Men. No, boys."

"Hm?" Lana asked from behind her sandwich.

Mrs. Martinez looked toward the kids. They were deep in conversation about some paranormal TV show that seemed to attract teens like ants to spilled soda, and thus oblivious. "My husband took the twins to his brother's while we're here. Look at this." She showed Lana her phone.

Lana found herself looking at a picture of a snow... penis. Yup, that was the whole shebang... sculpted out of snow like a snowman. She burst out laughing, almost choking on her food. "Oh, my *God*, warn me first?"

"Do I want to know?" Mel asked. Mrs. Martinez showed her, and Mel rolled her eyes and smirked. "Oh, boy. Creative!"

"These men," said Mrs. Martinez, putting her phone back in her handbag. "What we gonna do with them, right?"

Lana, who had no need for such answers anymore, sent Mel a conspiratorial grin—and Mel winked back! Lana's heartbeat raced as she realized that now Mel definitely knew she'd been flirting.

As the food on everyone's plates dwindled, Lana realized she was craving chocolate. She'd been up since far before dawn, driving the van from home so that Robin and Blanca could get settled in before the first rehearsal, and now she felt like a treat. "Does anyone want to split chocolate cake?"

"Ooh, you said my favorite magic word," said Mrs. Martinez.

"Can I have some?" asked Robin.

"Why don't we get one for the kids—*two* for the kids," Lana corrected herself, realizing how many of them there were, "and one for the three of us?"

"You two go on without me, I'm stuffed!" said Mel, ruling over her empty plate like the queen of full bellies.

But when the waitress came around to take dessert orders—"Sorry, we ran out of chocolate cake." She looked as if she expected to be sent to the firing squad.

"Oh, man!" Robin's shoulders slumped. "Can we get the peanut butter thing?"

"Peanut Butter Paradise?" The waitress wrote furiously, then looked expectantly at the adults.

"No, thanks," said Lana.

"Nah, I'm all right." Mrs. Martinez waved one hand as she fished around in her purse for her wallet. She pointed to Blanca. "Just the check. That one's mine. Oh, and put those two on my bill also."

Lana exclaimed, "Oh, you don't have to do that!"

"Pssh," said Mrs. Martinez. "You drove this morning. That was a lot of work!"

"Thanks."

"I hope they get the roads cleared soon," Mel commented, "before the hotel starts running out of more vital ingredients."

"Chocolate could be a vital ingredient," Lana quipped. "I've had a long day."

After the checks were paid, and everyone made quick detours to the ladies' room, the students returned to their respective ballrooms for the evening rehearsal. Lana curled up on the same seat as before. She tried to stay focused, but the music was too soothing this time and she'd done too much this morning starting too early. She slipped into a sleep that almost felt drugged, with the warm sounds of the string section washing all around her like a bubble bath.

Lana didn't know how long she'd slept, roused by the orchestra reaching a less quiet part of the piece. She noticed something in the seat beside her—it was a chocolate bar, on top of a piece of hotel stationery marked "—*M.*"

The next morning Lana rose to the realization that she'd developed a full-blown crush on the outgoing butch teacher. Excitement that she clicked with someone so cosmopolitan, so competent, and so *cute* propelled her out of bed feeling a little like she'd already drank some of the free in-room coffee whose smell now filled the room.

Melanie was proof that pixies weren't all twenty-three, Lana considered as she lathered hotel soap over herself in the shower. She remembered the playful look in her big dark eyes, and grinned so much she was glad only the shower curtain could see her.

She wasn't as lucky once she was dressed and admiring herself in the bathroom mirror. As she fussed over her blouse and looked at her reflection sideways—*my butt DOES look good in these jeans!*—she noticed Robin watching her. "This necklace goes, right? How do I look?"

Robin smirked. "Totally great. Hey," she added, drawing closer, "are you, like, interested in Ms. Feinberg?"

Lana broke into a smile broad enough to make her cheeks ache. "Hazards of having a genius kid." She adjusted the necklace. "How'd you know?"

Robin held up her phone. "I literally *just* had the exact same conversation with

Alexis about Tyler. She's been texting me selfies since before I woke up, like should she wear these earrings or those other ones. I'm pretty sure her phone autocompletes the name 'Tyler' when she types a T at this point."

"Seems like a nice kid," Lana mused. "Would that… be okay with you, hon? If I went out with Ms. Feinberg?"

"Yeah, I think she's neat!" said Robin. "She knows a lot."

A cloud dissipated in Lana's subconscious. "You don't get too much trouble from the other kids from me and your dad being out, do you?"

Robin made a face. "Please. I'm a band nerd. Anyone like that's already way off my radar."

A breakfast bar and banana later, Lana settled down in the rehearsal room ready for another day of motherly pride. Mel was nowhere to be found, so while the kids were getting their instruments out, Lana took out her phone and went back on Facebook to read more of those yummy compliments that were still pouring in on Robin's video.

We are so proud of you! You know, Stefan played in a rock band when he was your age.

That was Steve's mom. Lana felt a mix of awkwardness and relief, as she always did when interacting with her former in-laws these days. Both sets of fairly traditional parents were far more comfortable pretending the divorce had just been a parting of ways, and Lana was fine with that. The biggest load off her mind was that none of the four of them was taking it out on Robin or Nick.

Lana put away her phone, but Robin had a few measures of rest, so her eyes drifted instead to the first violins again. Watching their fingers dance around on the strips of black wood, shifting effortlessly, reminded her of lost moments. The smell of rosin, too, was bringing it all back.

"Biscotti for your thoughts?"

She turned to find Mel slipping into the seat next to her, wearing a stunning black blazer pantsuit and carrying one of those cheap totes that screamed "convention." Heat flushed Lana's cheeks. "Hey, thanks!" she whispered back, taking the cookie.

"It came from the convention center," Mel explained, taking utmost care to be as quiet as possible. "There's a café with pretty decent coffee right outside the exhibition hall. By the way, I talked to the staff, and they're used to this. During the winter, they always stock up when they're predicting a lot of snow, so it's not like we're gonna starve in here. Unless you still want that cake!"

Lana smiled so hard she felt like the points of her mouth were going to cut her cheeks. "I loved that chocolate bar last night, by the way. Thank you!"

"Good, that was the idea!" Mel smirked, and Lana liked the impish twinkle in her eye so much she had to remind herself that whipping out her phone to take a picture would be exceedingly socially bizarre. But *damn* if she didn't want to capture it and keep it like a butterfly in a jar.

"So does that mean we're still snowed in?"

"Well, apparently they got things cleared up in the early morning," said Mel, "but then it started all over again. So, yes. Sorry!"

"What about the kids at the other hotel?"

Mel made a face and shrugged. "Hopefully it'll clear up tonight. Or at least, by tomorrow morning. That's really the only day they have to be at the convention center." She relaxed into her chair and folded her hands under her chin, studying the musicians. The smile spreading across her face seemed to envelop the rest of her as she moved sinuously to the rhythm. "I love this piece."

"Yeah, the whole program is really fantastic," Lana agreed.

"I wish I were playing it with them," said Mel. "You think if I, you know, threw on a snapback and kept talking about vampires and werewolves on TV I could sneak in and pass as a high schooler?"

Lana chuckled. "Do you get to play in a symphony back home?"

Mel shook her head. "Not as much as I'd like. I take church gigs when I can get them, but between the orchestra and the chorus I pretty much don't have the time. Plus, I also have a chamber orchestra, about twenty of the county's best string players, that I'm also responsible for after hours."

"Wow."

"But I do get a chance to play sometimes— it's not a symphony, but I can usually find old-timey jams here and there. Weekends,

Monday nights, house parties on the holidays, or people's birthdays."

"What's old-timey?" asked Lana. Her throat was getting dry from all the whispering, so she took another sip of the English Breakfast at her feet.

"The predecessor of bluegrass," Mel explained. "Irish and Scottish fiddle met African banjo traditions in the Appalachians, and hundreds of years later, *voila*, you have fifteen people on folding chairs in someone's backyard."

Lana shivered. The initial rush of heat from Mel's arrival had succumbed to the hotel's inability to completely block out the winter outside. "I'm sorry; I have to go back to my room to get my sweater."

"I should head over to the junior group anyway," said Mel.

Dammit! Lana tried not to frown, but she was sure her disappointment was showing on her face. If only she hadn't been so determined to look her best for Mel, she wouldn't have left the frumpy cardigan up in the room in the first place.

"I can come with you if you want, so we can keep chatting without having to whisper," Mel continued. "When you come back down, I'll go over there."

"Sure!" *Whew*.

They made their way out of the room as quietly as possible and headed for the lobby elevators. "So, you took today and yesterday off work?" asked Mel as they stepped inside.

"Yeah, I work in the financial aid office at the university," said Lana.

"Oh, that's cool; you have a pretty normal schedule so you're off when the kids are off."

Lana nodded. "I actually like my job, too— and there's a pretty friendly atmosphere in the office. But you're right; not working in the evening means I can put the time into all that band mom stuff. Sometimes, that's almost like a second job."

"Who can sell the most lemon cookies?" Mel cracked.

"Guilty!" said Lana. "My office is still working on those things."

The elevator stopped. "So if you're off weekends," said Mel, stepping out, "you should come check out one of those jams I mentioned. Do you still have your violin?"

Lana's cheeks grew hot. "Yeah, I've still got it. Have my ex-husband's guitar, too."

"Bring it along!" said Mel. "Folk music is easy to pick up."

Lana swiped her keycard and opened the door to her room. "It's been a *reeeally* long time." She hunted for her sweater, glad that the room was relatively unembarrassing—not always a given where teenage girls were concerned. Wait, what was she even thinking? Anything they'd leave out, Mel had probably seen already. Well, that was a relief.

"If you'd rather just watch, that'd be fine, too," said Mel, her thumbs looped in the back pockets of her jeans. "We're more about sharing than audience, but there's usually somebody there not playing—either somebody's mom or partner. Free concert, when you think about it."

It wasn't until Lana caught sight of her own face in the mirror behind the bed that she realized she was frowning at that, too. She quickly smoothed her expression as she buttoned her sweater. "...yeah, I guess I'd better."

Mel flashed her a mischievous look from heavy-lidded, knowing eyes as she followed her out the door. "You *do* want to play."

Lana sighed. "I don't know. It's so easy for those kids down there—their fingers are like computers—they know where everything's supposed to go and I—it's been *twenty years*. If not more." The door clicked shut.

"Well, fine, you don't need to make up your mind now," said Mel. She sidled closer than casual as they waited for the elevator. "Either way, you'll come to the jam, and then maybe we can grab dinner?"

"Oh, I'm down for that!" said Lana enthusiastically, boarding the elevator. Good, at least Mel knew for sure that she was only reticent about this violin business, not dating women.

When they got back to the ballroom where the eleventh- and twelfth-grade orchestra rehearsed, the students were on break. "Hang on; I want to show you something."

"Hm?" Lana watched with interest as Mel approached one of the young violinists. It looked like there were some questions and then smiling, and then Mel took the girl's violin and bow.

Lana didn't know what to expect, but the sound that poured out when Mel began to play was rich and dark like that first bite of really good chocolate. She was shocked into silence, captivated by the simple, wistful melody. At some point, she realized her mouth was hanging open a little, and she closed it with some embarrassment, licking her lips.

Some of the kids watched, too. Another violinist joined in, and Lana had to admit that a part of her was aching to join them. The melody didn't *sound* hard… still, something held her back. She was acutely aware of an invisible wall between her and these kids, maybe between her and Mel as well. She didn't trust that her fingers would know what to do, and she was scared that if she tried to tell them, they wouldn't listen.

"Mom! Mom, mom, mom, we got a problem."

Lana's mind snapped instantly to Robin, the violinist and the lover sitting down to let the Mom take over again. "Honey?"

"Out in the hallway." Robin practically dragged her out by the sleeve of her sweater.

In the hallway, surrounded by other kids Lana hoped were her friends, Alexis was slumped over on the floor, holding her head in her hands. "I am such a fucking idiot; I'm gonna die…"

"What happened?" asked Lana.

Alexis looked up, revealing a very red face. "I forgot to take my allergy meds this morning, so I tried to take them just now while I was going to the bathroom. But I dropped them all in the toilet. I already skipped today. If I skip tomorrow I'm gonna get a death-migraine and won't be able to play. Oh, my God, I can't believe this…"

"And nobody else has any," Robin volunteered. "We already asked."

Lana squeezed her shoulder. "Okay, we can fix this. I think there's a Walgreens on the corner."

"It's snowing again, though," said a kid whose name Lana didn't know.

"That's okay," said Lana, "I brought my ski jacket."

"You'll walk me to the Walgreens after rehearsal?" Alexis's face looked like the sun peeking through clouds.

"Of course. We can't have you missing your concert! Not after all that work!"

"I was afraid to ask Madison's mom," said Alexis. "She's the one chaperoning me and I'm honest to God scared of her. She would yell at me and it's not even her money."

Lana brushed her hair out of her face. "I'll be here during the rehearsal, and then afterward just come up to the room with us so I can get my jacket, okay?"

"Thanks so much, Ms. Novak. You are seriously the best."

"My mom's a rock star," beamed Robin.

A few hours later, Lana led a gaggle of teenage girls back to her hotel room. "Oh, wow, Ms. Novak, that coat's amazing!" Alexis exclaimed when she saw Lana's shimmery blue ski jacket. The fabric was metameric, and it shone green and purple in some places when the light hit it just right.

"I know, isn't this great?" Lana checked the jacket's pockets to make sure her gloves and scarf were still there, then grabbed the hat Robin had knitted her for Christmas off the dresser. "I hope you brought a good jacket. We can hit your room for it on the way down."

Alexis looked distraught. "But what about Madison's mom? She's gonna… like…"

"She's not *your* mom," Lana shook her head in frustration. "She doesn't really have any right to talk to you like that, anyway. She can just… Look, I'll be with you. Just run in, get the jacket, and leave. If she asks where you're going, tell her the truth and remember that no matter how she responds, it's *none of her business*. I'll be in the hallway in case anything happens."

"Okay." Alexis looked sick, but gave Lana a half smile.

"Not you, Robin." Lana realized Robin was putting on her own coat. "I don't want you out there in the snow, not the day before a concert. Your lungs are part of your instrument."

"Can we go to the dealer's room?" Robin asked.

"You mean the exhibition hall? Yes, but stay together and keep your phones where you can hear me so I can call when I'm on my way back. *Stay together*."

Robin clamped her hand on Blanca's wrist. "Buddy system!"

Amazing how much easier it is to tell other people not to be scared of things, Lana observed as she rode the elevator with Alexis down to the other floor, *than to convince yourself not to be scared*. And honestly, a cranky snob with a hair-trigger temper like Mrs. Woods did sound scarier than picking up a violin again. So why was she so nervous about it?

Her mind flipped to a memory of the year she'd taken dance as a youngster, starting later than the other girls. It was hard to erase the awkwardness of being the biggest elf in the Christmas show—even though it wasn't her fault she was a beginner at ten instead of five like everyone else. She might have stuck with dancing if more of the girls at her level were her age.

Was that it? Was she reticent to pick up the bow again and then be the forty-three-year-old woman who sounded as halting as some of Mel's students—the ones who weren't good enough to be here at All-State?

Maybe she was just afraid of looking inept in front of Mel. Luckily, Mel was the kind of universally friendly person who didn't seem like she'd make a big deal out of mess-ups.

She waited in the hallway outside Alexis's room, giving herself the kind of pep talk she'd have given one of the girls.

Alexis finally emerged, bundled into a puffy coat with a university logo, and grinning. "She's not there!"

"Phase one, complete," said Lana as they headed back to the elevator. "All aboard for the Polar Express to Walgreens!"

The first blast of icy air outside the hotel's front door assaulted Lana's face like knives. She'd covered as much as humanly possible, with her scarf wrapped around her cheeks and chin and then tucked into her pulled-up collar, and her hat pulled low over her ears. But nothing could completely block out the wet, cutting chill.

"You okay?" she called out.

"This suuuucks," was Alexis's response. "I'm so sorry for you having to come out here like this with me."

"It's an adventure!" Lana told her. "Something for you to tell your kids someday." She lifted her boot as high as she could to take the next step into the high drifts of snow. When she put it down again it sank disconcertingly into the fluffy flakes. "Watch your step."

"Yeah."

Lana fixed her sight on the bright red Walgreens sign, barely visible in the white-gray swirl. Snow stopped being fun past high school, she reflected, burying her gloved hands in her pockets. "Speaking of adventures, how did you manage to drop your pills in the toilet in the first place?”

“Um,” said Alexis, continuing her slow, stomping march across the snowbank. “I was kind of… texting.”

“You took your phone out in the ladies’ room? You’re lucky you didn’t drop *that* in the toilet!” *Teenagers*, Lana thought to herself, before a little voice reminded her that she’d shivered through the first half of Robin’s morning rehearsal without her sweater because it wasn’t Mel-worthy.

“Oh, my God, my mom would *kill me*,” said Alexis. “Yeah, I know it was kinda dumb but things might be going somewhere with Tyler and I couldn’t wait to see his next message.”

“Well, that’s good, anyway?” Trust a boy Tyler’s age to feel more comfortable talking about his feelings via text message.

“Yeah! I feel good about it,” said Alexis. “We’re supposed to go see the new

Captain Werewolf movie next weekend together."

"Congratulations!"

Lana and Alexis fought the snow together until they reached the drugstore, where they killed several more minutes inside, just to enjoy the warmth. "We're on our way back," Lana told Robin into a cell that felt uncomfortable against her cold-stained cheek.

"Cool," said Robin. "How is it out there?"

"You know that year you played the Waltz of the Snowflakes from *Nutcracker* for the Christmas concert?" Lana shifted out of the doorway to let another bundled-up soul exit. "Not that. Not even close. It's like a science fiction movie."

"Don't freeze," said Robin.

"See you soon."

On the way back, being forced to lift her boot-heavy feet higher than usual in order to take the next step into the drifts began to make her knees hurt. To distract herself, she thought of Mel playing that song—the simple waltz from before. She didn't know why, but it reminded her of bittersweet movies about immigrants longing for their home country. Naturally, as the child of immigrants she'd been exposed to a fair number of those her whole life.

Hearing it in her mind made her fingers, trapped inside her fists inside gloves inside pockets and close against her body, unconsciously start trying out what might be the positions for the song.

Immigrants thinking of a far-off time and place… was that what violin was, to her? A land across the ocean, full of complex beauty and history?

The hotel lobby beckoned invitingly with its promise of warmth and lack of frozen rain attacking one's eyelashes. Lana and Alexis hurried inside to find Robin and Melanie waiting for them.

"Supermom!" Robin pumped both fists straight in the air, before making an octopus out of her hand to squish Alexis's head playfully.

Mel held out an insulated paper cup. "I bet you need this."

Lana took it carefully in her still-gloved hand. Hot, spiced apple cider! She enjoyed the smell and the warm steam against her nose for a moment before taking a sip, then rested the cup against her cheek. "Wow, thanks! You're right, that's perfect. How did you know?"

"Robin found me at one of the sheet music booths and told me where you were. Here, take those off." Mel took Lana's free hand and peeled off her glove. Lana, still in her coat, flushed warmly at the first time their hands met. Mel's fingers were gentle and guiding on hers, steering her bare hand around the cup she held in her gloved one. Intense heat from the cider caressed her palm. "Isn't that just what your fingers need after being out there? Even in gloves it's hard not to feel like there's ice *inside* your body after being out there."

"This is just about my favorite way to eat apples," said Lana, unable to take her eyes away from Mel's hospitable smile, and reveling in their impromptu hand-holding.

Mel squeezed Lana's hand against the cup and then relinquished it to fish a business card holder out of her convention bag. "Hey, I have to go to a seminar, but call me after the afternoon rehearsal and I'll join up with you all for dinner." She pressed her card into Lana's waiting hand.

"Thanks again for the apple cider," Lana said through smiles and fluttering eyelashes.

Dinner was another group affair, even larger this time, and Mel spent most of it entertaining all the students present with unusual stories from the lives of composers. "Of course, none of that's quite as awful as Jean-Baptiste Lully, who accidentally killed himself with his own baton."

"You're shitting me," said Tyler. "*Dammit!*" He smacked his face.

Mel rolled her eyes and looked at him with stern affection. "Tyler, I don't care if you curse, as long as you practice. You can swear every other word for all I care but you better nail that Saint-Saëns."

"You got it, Ms. Feinberg!"

"What happened with the baton?" asked Blanca. "Was it on purpose?"

"Nope!" said Mel. "Back then, batons were these big heavy—" She mimed banging a pole on the ground. "He hit himself in the foot and died of gangrene."

Robin's eyes grew wide. "That's so sad!"

"So nowadays, if my baton goes flying across the room and lands in the violas, I just think, hey, it's not as bad as it could be."

Mel's amazing with kids, Lana observed. She wondered how Nick would take to her. Toying with her straw, she knew she was getting ahead of herself, but it was a safer train of thought than some of the others she could have followed in front of all these people. Mel looked like a dapper butch goddess in her crisp blazer, and the hot-cider-hand-holding incident made Lana want more warm touches.

She got her wish later on. The students had the night off before their big concert, and several of them had aggregated, with the moms, in one of the hotel rooms to watch a movie. The young musicians were enraptured by the turbulent love life of composer Franz Liszt; most of them had seen the movie at least once if not more, and they kept a running commentary on their favorite parts—which meant that Mel and Lana weren't disturbing anyone by chatting quietly.

"My neck aches a little from being out in that mess out there," said Lana. The window shade was drawn back on one side, revealing a hazy pink glow past which faint snowflakes flitted. Safe on the other side of the thick glass, they seemed misleadingly gentle.

"C'mere. I'll see what I can do." Mel's fingertips and thumb sent happy ribbons of promise down Lana's body.

"Thanks! Oh, yeah, that really does help." Lana felt such relief at being able to enjoy moments like this, finally, after decades of silence and stifling herself. She wasn't that religious, but a powerful gratitude rocked her soul and called for silent prayer. "I loved that song you were playing earlier this morning in the rehearsal room."

"Oh, thanks!" said Mel. "It's just a folk tune. It's called 'Si Bheag Si Mhor.'"

Lana couldn't place the unfamiliar syllables. "Is that a Jewish thing?" she hazarded.

Mel chuckled. "No, it's Irish. But you guessed right on Feinberg."

"Any idea what the name means?" Lana leaned into the neck massage, savoring each moment.

"Something about two hills where two warriors were buried, and their ghosts kept on fighting."

"Really? It sounds so gentle and sweet."

"Old-timey names are all over the place," said Mel. "People make jokes that the only reason we even have them is to tell the tunes apart. That's how we wind up with stuff like 'Cluck, Old Hen' and 'Tater Patch'."

"I'm sorry I had to leave in the middle of She... of the Irish thing, but that's when Alexis was having her little emergency," said Lana. "I'd love to hear it again, really *listen* to it."

"Yeah?" Mel looked around the room. "You think there's enough adults in here without us, if we left for a few minutes?"

"What, you mean, now?" Besides Blanca's mom, Lana counted two other chaperones in the room. "I think we should be able to pop out... You brought your violin to the conference?"

"Nope!"

"Then what are you gonna..."

"I'll improvise!"

Lana blinked, but Mel seemed perpetually unafraid, and being around her energized Lana. The feeling rising in her chest reminded her of the swarm of bubbles flowing to the top of a glass of club soda. "I can't wait to see how you're gonna pull this off," she said as she stood up.

"Hey, we'll be right back, okay?" Mel told the room. "You'll be fine for a few moments if we duck out? We're gonna go stretch our legs."

"Fine, fine," said Mrs. Martinez with a smile, before going back to her animated conversation with the other two moms.

Lana followed through the hallway as Mel, who seemed like Peter Pan in a blazer with her spontaneous energy, led her to a room around the corner. She stood with her hands resting on her hips as Mel knocked. "Student's room," the teacher explained.

Lana smiled, but nobody answered the door. "Oh, well!" said Mel. "Next stop!"

They took an elevator to another floor and tried another room, but nobody was there, either. Back to the elevator. Mel didn't look disappointed by their striking out— her face was lit up by the adventure.

"So, do you like Thai? There's a new place that opened up across the street from Tulip Tree and I haven't had anything bad there yet."

"Sure, I'd love to try it!" said Lana as the elevator doors opened.

At the next room, somebody finally came to the door—but it was the other student in the room, not the violinist, and Mel understood completely that she didn't want to lend out someone else's instrument without their permission. "These aren't all *your* students, are they?" Lana furrowed her brow, trying to remember what Mel said earlier about who was here representing Tulip Tree strings.

"No, some of them are from that chamber group."

"Oh, right! I'd like to hear them play sometime."

Mel hurried down the corridor. "Next month on the 8th, Tchaikovsky Serenade for Strings."

Lana didn't want to ask *What if we don't find a violin?* She was afraid that would somehow break the spell.

The next room was another nobody there—"Everyone's probably at the convention center or eating dinner," Mel mused—but at the fifth room they struck gold.

"Sure, but you'll bring it back in a few minutes, right?" The gangly young man at the door handed his case over to Mel.

"Definitely, safe and sound."

Mel's room was a warm and golden place under the light of the single lamp she switched on when they entered. The effect was enhanced by the unexpected fragrance of pumpkin-spice-something. "Ooh, it smells good in here," Lana remarked, trying to look around without being too snoopy.

"It's my little air freshener friend," said Mel, putting the violin case on the extra bed. She unzipped it from both directions at once. "I like to put that scent in places that become home. It's sort of a mental health thing. Hope it's okay?"

"Oh, yeah! That's a great smell." Lana caught the comment as the first mention of any vulnerability in Mel's superwoman image, and treasured the feeling of being trusted. But then, wasn't speaking so openly just yet another sign of Mel's confidence and poise? "If you like it, you'll love what happens to my house just before the band bake-sales."

"Maybe I should come over and practice." Mel tightened the bow, then lifted the violin to her shoulder.

Sitting on the bed with her sock-clad feet in front of her, Lana watched Mel admiringly. Once again, she began to play the lilting dance from that morning. With clever finger tricks, she made it sound what Lana started to think of as "extra Irish". It was almost as if Mel were flirting with some of the notes instead of simply playing them.

When Mel stopped, Lana assumed she was going to adjust her bow again or maybe change tunes. Instead, she walked to the bed and nudged Lana's thigh with her knee. "Move over."

"Huh?"

Mel let her butt do the talking, and Lana had no choice but to scoot. She felt delightfully cozy, sidled up to Mel like this, but what was going on? Mel was still holding the violin.

—No, she wasn't.

Lana found herself holding the slim wooden sculpture without realizing how it had happened. "I can't—this belongs to somebody else—"

"I've got you covered." Mel's voice was a throaty, soothing caress. "I'm right here." She pressed the bow into Lana's right hand.

Lana drew the bow across the strings. A brilliant fifth rang out, D and A, and Lana vibrated along with them. "Oh."

"Yes."

"But I don't remember anything."

"Try what I just played."

Lana shook her head. "I only heard it today!"

"Would it help if you had music? Do you remember?"

"I think I might... from helping Robin, at the piano."

Mel then proceeded to blow Lana's mind by sliding open the drawer that usually only held Gideon Bibles and suggestions for where to order pizza, if it wasn't snowing its ass off, and retrieving a sheet of paper. "Here."

"You wrote it out?" Lana's eyes bugged. There it was—handwritten in neat blue pen.

"Helped me stay focused during that seminar." Mel placed the paper delicately over Lana's thighs. "Can you see, or do you want me to hold it?"

"I'd rather you keep spotting me," Lana said quickly. "This still isn't my violin."

Mel nodded. "*La la laaaa la la laaaa la la la laaaa la laaaa,*" she sang, pointing. Her clear voice was a whole new pleasure. "Right here."

Lana took a deep breath, placed her left ring finger on the A string, lifted the bow, and landed.

D, E, F#—, E, D, D—, E, D, A, B—, A, F#—...

The notes actually sounded like notes! The violin sounded like a violin! Her sound was awkward, but it only enhanced the rustic folk tune. It's not like this was Mendelssohn or something. Her fingers felt raw and naked, pressed up against taut metal like that for the first time in decades, but it didn't hurt.

Lana knew she didn't sound like Mel, or even like Mel's students, but she was making music. The song that had wrapped itself around her heart like a ribbon ever since first meeting Mel—no, before, ever since coming out and deciding to be her own brave self—was finally escaping with each breath, confined no longer.

She shot a glance at Mel, falling into those big dark eyes, that welcoming smile. Mel nodded slowly and squeezed Lana's knee. Her head moved subtly in time with the music, and then Lana realized she was humming along—in harmony.

Too much good. Tears began to blur the music. Lana blinked them away and kept going.

After a few rounds, she put the violin down and breathed deeply.

"So, yeah," said Mel.

They looked at each other, grinning and glowing.

Lana giggled from sheer emotion. "What else you got?"

"Fiddle tunes, or do you want me to kiss you?"

"Both. Everything." Lana looked up at the ceiling, almost as if seeing the black sky beyond it with the snow cleared and the stars out.

"Let me move this." Mel rescued the violin from Lana's reverent hands, placing it carefully on the nightstand with the bow beside it. Then she turned back to Lana and brushed a lock of hair back over her shoulder. "You're more fearless than you think you are."

"Meeting you makes me stop feeling bad for waiting so long." And it was Lana who moved forward first, closing her eyes and tilting her head as naturally as if this weren't the first time she was kissing in her native language.

Their hands held each other's gently as they kissed, the sense of peace and rightness flowing through the room along with the baking spices. Maybe it was Lana's imagination, but she thought she

heard the violin's strings resonating in
harmony.

END

♫

Reference playlist:
Pines of Rome, Ottorino Respighi. Third movement, "Pines of the Janiculum"
Pines of Rome, Ottorino Respighi. Fourth movement, "Pines of the Appian Way"
Prelude to the Afternoon of a Faun, Claude Debussy
Shibeg Shimore, Turlough O'Carolan/traditional

Shira Glassman is a bi Jewish violinist from Florida. She eats, breathes, and sleeps violin, but what the hell is "snow"?

If you liked Shira Glassman's *Fearless*, leaving a review is probably a mitzvah. If you want more fiction by Ms. Glassman focused on music, musicians, and love between women, *A Harvest of Ripe Figs*, about a stolen violin, is a full-length fantasy cozy.

Shira Glassman is a bisexual Jewish violinist living in Florida. Her books, inspired by her heritage, upbringing, present life, and favorite operas, have made the finals of both the Bi Book Awards and the Golden Crown Literary Society awards in more than one year. She learned to knit from her grandmother and is grateful for all the friends and artistic fulfillment it has brought her.

Shira Glassman online:
Blog: http://shiraglassman.wordpress.com
Facebook:
http://www.facebook.com/ShiraGlassman
Goodreads:
https://www.goodreads.com/author/show/
7234426.Shira_Glassman
Twitter:
http://www.twitter.com/shiraglassman

If you liked *Knit One, Girl Two* or *Fearless*, leaving a review is probably a mitzvah.

Also by Shira Glassman:

The Mangoverse:
The Second Mango
Climbing the Date Palm
A Harvest of Ripe Figs
The Olive Conspiracy
Tales from Perach/Tales from Outer Lands*
**excerpted on next page*

Additional stories about women with women:
Cinnamon Blade: Knife in Shining Armor
Wet Nails
Eitan's Chord

Short stories featuring Jewish m/f romance:
Gifts of Spring
Lioness in Blue
A Man of Taste

Other short stories:
The Artist and the Devil
When Daisies Choose a Vase
Treasure Hunt

And now some recommendations for other people's excellent f/f fiction!

Daughter of Mystery by Heather Rose Jones
Poppy Jenkins by Clare Ashton
Out on Good Behavior by Dahlia Adler
That Could Be Enough by Alyssa Cole
Wrong Number, Right Woman by Jae
Moon-Bright Tides by RoAnna Sylver
The Cybernetic Tea Shop by Meredith Katz

Recommendations for Jewish fiction

The Golem and the Jinni by Helene Wecker
The Vanisher Variations by Libi Astaire
Miss Jacobson's Journey by Carola Dunn
The Upside of Unrequited by Becky
Albertalli

and for Jewish f/f, in loving memory

Eight Kinky Nights by Xan West z"L

by **Shira Glassman**

excerpted story:
"Your Name is Love"

This is a work of fiction. Names, characters, places, and incidents are either the product of the author's imagination or are used fictitiously, and any resemblance to any persons, dragons, or cats, living or dead, business establishments, events, or locales is entirely coincidental.

Tales of Perach by Shira Glassman, edited by Jaymi Lynn
"Your Name is Love"
An energetic royal guard takes her artist wife on a scavenger hunt around the city so she can stop having artist's block about the lesbian graphic novel she's supposed to make for the queen.

"Dayenu" song verse from the Passover Haggadah, sourced from the public domain.

Appreciation to J.L. Douglas for beta-reading. All remaining errors are mine.

Your Name is Love

Cast: Hadar/Halleli from *The Olive Conspiracy*

Rededicated in 2021 in loving memory to Corey/Xan West (z'L), in gratitude for 2017.

"Whoo!" Hadar came smashing across the garden, her face glowing and her sweaty under-tunic sticking to her wiry, muscled frame. She twirled the outer portion of her guard uniform from two fingers. "Free for the rest of the day! Hey, look, it's the prettiest girl in the palace. Guess what? I beat my personal best today."

"That's terrific! I'm so proud of you." Halleli, who had looked up at the first familiar noise, put her sketchpad on the ground beside her and stood up for a kiss.

"You smell like garlic," Hadar blurted out before Halleli could say anything. "Maybe I should snarf you up for dinner."

Halleli giggled as heat flushed her cheeks. "Yael needed extra help in the back today to get ready for a bar mitzvah catering job. Is it really bad? I can—"

"Why would it be bad? Everybody likes garlic! Who doesn't like garlic?"

"I might be able to get some rosewater from the quee—"

"It's fine, I like it." Hadar ran her hands down Halleli's upper arms. "I need to jump in the creek before dinner. You coming?"

"Sure! I already washed up, but I'll hang out." Halleli bent down to retrieve her art supplies and then followed the cutest butch in the world toward the creek behind the palace.

Hadar, naked in the water, reached down to scrub dead skin off her foot. "You still working on that drawing with Olive and the flowers?" Olive was their little black kitten, a gift from the queen's bodyguard, who was Hadar's boss.

"It's somewhere," said Halleli, holding her left hand out in front of her and studying it critically. "This one's for the queen."

"More family portraits?"

Halleli shook her head. "You remember I told you that when she was growing up she got into her father's books and found art of women like us, women together in couples?"

"Yeah, but you said it was all shit."

"It was insulting. I saw some of it myself and she was right—it's not us. It's not for us. It has nothing to do with us. It's so obvious the women are being drawn for the audience and aren't paying any attention to each other, and when the pictures got... graphic... that's not how it... you don't..."

"So, lemme guess—she's got you drawing something better."

"Exactly! She wants me to make her a codex—maybe even more, if this one works out. With pictures, that tell a story, and dialogue written in."

"So how's it going?"

Halleli's face twisted. "Eh, I've done so much better. If you want to see what I've got so far —"

Hadar waded to the edge of the water and peered over. "Looks pretty good to me. Who are they supposed to be?"

"I don't know. I just feel like they're— wooden. Flat."

Hadar hopped around, creating complex ripples in the water. "Make something up, then."

"That's the problem," said Halleli. "I haven't made up any new stories in ages."

"Are you sad? Do you need hugs?"

"I always need hugs. But it's not really that, it's…" Halleli paused, her pencil resting against her lip. "I feel like my mind is out of ideas, or out of… out of whatever ideas are made with. Like it's having trouble finding the raw materials."

"Maybe you're working too hard." Hadar patted the water with the flats of her hands in a series of tiny, controlled splats.

"That's part of it," said Halleli. "I love working at the restaurant—Yael's very nice to me, and the customers always gush over their portraits. But there's no *thinking* time. You can't hide inside yourself working in a kitchen. And we don't live on our own anymore. I can go hide in our quarters if I want to think something through, but that's not as inspiring as being out in the open."

"I think I have an idea," said Hadar.

"A story idea for my art for the queen?"

"No, an idea for an adventure," Hadar said. "We'd have to both have the afternoon off at the same time though."

"I'm working all day tomorrow and the next day, but right after that I'm only on until the end of the lunch rush."

"That should work!" said Hadar, stepping out of the water and onto the soft grass of the bank. She began to dry her shimmering, golden-brown skin with a piece of cotton cloth.

"What are we going to go do?" asked Halleli, intrigued.

Hadar pulled a clean tunic over her head and toweled off her hair with a flourish. "It's a surprise!"

Three days later, Halleli hurried home from the restaurant full of anticipation. Chopping vegetables, carrying plates, and sketching patrons had left little time in her morning for conjecture. But now in these last few minutes before Hadar appeared, while Halleli tied her hair behind a fresh scarf that didn't smell like kitchen grease, she reveled in the unknown. Was Hadar taking her shopping? Were they going out beyond the city to look for wild flying goats? Maybe they were going to the other side of town, to the river docks, to watch the longshoremen unloading cargo ships.

From her perch at the foot of their bed, Olive the kitten chirped and rolled onto her side. "Aww, who's cute? *Who's cute?*" Halleli was still petting her when Hadar appeared in the doorway. "Hey!"

"You ready?" Hadar grinned. She had

already changed into her civilian clothes.

Halleli nodded. "Hurray, I finally get to find out what you've been up to!"

"I hope you like it." Still beaming, Hadar knocked her fists together with nervous energy. "Look under your pillow."

Halleli furrowed her brow, then slid her hand between the pillow and the sheet. She was surprised to find a paper there. That hadn't been there last night, or it would have crinkled. "What's this?"

"I made you a scavenger hunt," said Hadar. "That's the first clue."

Halleli's mouth dropped open and she glowed, impressed. This was not to be *one* adventure, but several! A swirl of glee rose within her. "Thank you!" She unfolded the paper and read from it, in Hadar's writing. "*The queen's sanctuary. Are we even allowed in there?"

Hadar jumped from foot to foot. "You

have to go and see! I'm not helping. I'm just along for the ride."

 With a final caress of Olive's fuzzy face, Halleli led Hadar from the room and shut the door. They waved hello to some on-duty guards as they crossed the courtyard to the royal suites, and ducked to the side for a moment to avoid a pair of laundresses scurrying past with armfuls of clean sheets.

 Halleli could see the queen in her bedroom through the open doorway when they arrived. Queen Shulamit bustled around gathering and sorting documents, the baby princess strapped to her chest in a golden sling. She lifted a hand in greeting when she saw the other women. "Spending the afternoon off together?"

 "Yes, Majesty!" said Halleli, her insides pleasantly warm. "Hadar made me a scavenger hunt, and I think the first clue leads here."

Queen Shulamit's heavy eyebrows jutted forward. "In here?" She looked toward Hadar. "Did one of the maids hide it?"

"No, no—" Hadar drummed her fingers on her other hand. "Sorry, Majesty. Halleli, it's not in here. I should have said something before we bothered you."

"It's no bother! I think this is really sweet, that you made clues for her. I just don't know anything about it."

"I'm sorry," said Halleli, her cheeks hot with embarrassment. "I just thought it had to be here."

Queen Shulamit reached toward her. "Can I see the clue?" When she read it, her face spread into a burst of a smile. "Oh! I see why you came here, but I know what Hadar meant."

Halleli's eyelashes fluttered. "But you have only one bedroom, and the whole

214

palace is your home."

"Think about what the clue would mean," said the queen, "if it were *you* she was talking about. Anyway, good luck and have fun!" She retreated back into the sumptuous little bedroom, leaving Hadar and Halleli outside.

"If it were me…" Halleli licked her lips. "*My* sanctuary. Well, I mean, there's our room, but it still doesn't feel like home yet… home is…" She turned to face Hadar, realization pouring into her. "Home is *you*. Home is you, you're my sanctuary, and Aviva has the second clue!"

Hadar stuck her tongue out at her. "I was talking about the kitchen-house, since she eats in there except Shabbat and holidays, but close enough."

"Oh, that makes sense."

The kitchen-house of the queen's wife did indeed look every bit the hidden royal sanctuary as they approached, with its cream-colored walls peeking out from behind trellises of passion vine and cucumber. Halleli was momentarily distracted by the assortment of herbs growing on both sides of the path to the door—mint, cilantro, lemongrass, and a basil bush so leafy and lush she almost wanted to lie down in it like it was a pillow.

 The door burst open and Aviva emerged holding a pair of clippers. "Oh, you're home already!"

 Halleli nodded. "Hadar's taking me on an adventure."

 "Yes, I know," said Aviva with a twinkle in her eye as she snipped and collected bits of lemongrass and cilantro. "I have the next clue inside waiting for you."

 "We're allowed to come in?" Halleli's cheeks flushed and she felt shy.

 "You both have to promise that you're not

bread," said Aviva with just the *hint* of a smile on her pretty face. "Or chickens."

"Not today, anyway!" said Hadar, and Halleli giggled.

They followed Aviva inside. "Ooh, what are you working on?" Halleli asked when she saw the pile of pecan shells.

"Sweet potato pie," said Aviva, "with a pecan crust."

"So the whole crust is nuts? Neat!" said Hadar.

"That sounds healthier than a regular crust anyway," said Halleli.

"Here, try some!" Aviva held out tiny bites to each of them.

"It's wonderful," Halleli breathed once her mouth wasn't full of sweet, sticky nuts.

"Kinda like baklava," Hadar said through munches.

"Here's your clue, by the way," said Aviva, handing over a folded piece of paper. "Sorry about the, um, that one looks like it's probably goat grease. And... black beans."

"Don't worry about it," said Halleli. Her heart was still fluttering slightly from being in a place *this important*, at least for a few minutes. The queen might be her friend, but she was still very conscious of the difference in their life circumstances.

"That sounds really good though," said Hadar. "Makes me want to lick the clue!"

Halleli smiled nervously at the comment and unfolded the paper. "'You can't buy sunshine, except from her.' Buy sunshine? Oh! I know! The juice stand at the entrance to the marketplace!"

"And it's orange season, so it really does taste like sunshine," Aviva affirmed as she scraped nut shells into her compost bin.

Of course the young ladies had to buy juice the minute they arrived at the woman's stall; one couldn't be surrounded by piles of fresh, glowing oranges like that without being tempted. They hadn't brought cups with them, so they had to drink them while standing there, but Auntie Juice was used to it and didn't mind. She stood at her countertop, squeezing more fruit against her special bowl as she watched them with a face full of satisfaction.

"Who was it who first said this is the taste of sunshine?" Halleli asked between sips.

Hadar shrugged. "My sister, but so did your dad, and Eliana, and that traveling salesman peddling blankets."

"I remember him!" Halleli exclaimed. "He said it was what really made him feel like he'd arrived in Perach."

"That's why I have free samples," said Auntie Juice. "Once they taste it, travelers always want a cup. It's irresistible!"

"Thank you for the juice," said Halleli, setting the cup down and folding her hands respectfully. "Do you have the next clue for me?"

"Now where did I…?" Auntie Juice rummaged around in both pockets of her apron, then looked behind a stack of fruit crates. "Oh! Here."

"Thank you!" Halleli straightened out the paper, which was crumpled and a little juice-speckled. "'It's bad to break things, but it's good to break these. In some cases it's all they're good for.' Um… breaking… promises… dates… no, that's still bad. Breaking dawn? I'd think you wanted me to watch the sun come up with you but it's afternoon."

Hadar watched this musing monologue with merry eyes as she danced around a little in front of the stall.

"Oh!" Halleli exclaimed suddenly. "Eggs! Of course."

Hadar threw up her hands in celebration.

"Are they all going to be food?" Halleli asked.

Hadar grinned sheepishly. "No, I must have been hungry when I started making up clues. But I'm not saying they're *not* food—I don't want to give you too many hints."

"You two are cute," said Auntie Juice.

"Thank you," said Halleli, looking at the ground and slinking backward slightly until her shadow overlapped with Hadar's. But she was smiling.

Several people in the marketplace sold eggs, but Halleli knew Hadar was talking about the stall they usually passed on the way to their favorite tiny public park, which was only big enough to hold one bench and two rosebushes. The egg man was explaining something to a customer when they arrived, and they waited their turn.

"Well, if you *say* so," said the man buying the eggs. He looked confused. "But I'll see what my wife says when I bring them home."

"I *promise* the brown shell doesn't mean the chickens are getting too much sun." The egg man waved in farewell, his face a study in controlled exasperation. Then he turned toward Hadar. "Oh, it's you!"

"Too much sun?" asked Hadar. "That's a new one."

"Hey, there are no silly questions—just silly customers." The egg man retrieved a strangely folded paper from beneath one of his egg baskets. "Hope it's okay that I did that. Have to keep my hands busy and I didn't realize that wasn't one of mine."

"Oh, that's so cute, you made a flower out of it!" gasped Halleli in delight.

"That's great!" said Hadar. "I want to learn to do that. I can't keep still either, and that sounds like a really fun way to handle it." She studied the flower, then presented it to Halleli with a gallant flourish.

"I like this adventure you cooked up," said the egg man. "This is your sister, right?"

Halleli felt fire in her cheeks and she wanted to fade into the trees, but Hadar responded promptly. "No, this is my wife. We're like the queen."

"Oh, right, I didn't know that." The egg man nodded. "You look alike."

"No, we don't," Hadar whispered in Halleli's ear after they'd walked away.

"I'm so glad Queen Shulamit is so open and straightforward about her life and family," Halleli murmured in response. "It makes things so much easier to explain."

Their move to the big city had meant introductions happened all the time now, instead of the small farming village where they'd lived together for the past few years where everyone knew they were a couple without having to talk about it. If the queen had not also been drawn to women, Halleli was *sure* things would be more difficult.

"Definitely. Read your clue, love!"

"But I'll have to ruin the flower."

"I'll learn to make my own. Then you won't be able to stop me and our room will be waist-deep in 'em."

Halleli giggled, then read. "'He uses fire, rock, and water to make things.' That sounds... like God. Is the clue at the synagogue?"

Hadar smirked. "I totally wasn't reading that much into it—try less poetic and more literal."

Halleli's eyelashes fluttered, her mind stuck in the mud.

"But," Hadar added as she took her by the hand, no doubt after seeing the frown, "I like the idea, and I bet you'll turn it into something with your art or writing."

"Be careful," said Halleli as grains of pride gathered. "If the queen saw me do something like that she might make me illustrate the whole Tanakh!"

"Starting with the Book of Esther," said Hadar.

"I'm already working on that."

"She's predictable!"

"So, who literally makes things out of fire? The potter needs fire to harden the pots… and earth to make the pots with…"

"I guess my clue was a little too broad."

"It's not the potter?" Halleli asked. "Is it more food?"

Hadar shook her head emphatically.

A cry from the marketplace cut through the chatter. "Toss the horseshoe 'round the pole and win a prize!"

"Oh, it's the *blacksmith*!" Halleli clapped her hands.

"Yay!"

They hurried off toward the forge.

Halleli stopped when she saw a small crowd gathered around a man in sparkly, purple clothing. "Ooh, what's he doing?"

"Looks like magic tricks." Hadar hovered close to her, one hand protectively close to her back.

The man, an athletic fortyish with a braided beard, was holding up a coin to those watching. He showed one side, then the other, before holding out his hand in invitation for audience volunteers. Small children in the front hopped up and down, and he chose one of them. Handing the coin to the youngster with instructions to keep it tightly in one fist, he then proceeded to stand on his head to scattered applause and children's laughter.

He then asked for a second volunteer. This time, he extended his hand to an old woman clutching a basket of vegetables. Before the crowd's eyes, that hand waved in the air and suddenly held a blooming lily. "Ooh!" rose through the audience. The old woman's face crinkled with delight.

"Wait, the flower isn't free!" the magician said dramatically. "You must pay me. Use the coin I gave the little one—it's in your vegetables."

"It is?" she asked in wonder. "Oh, my goodness, it is!" And she handed it over for him to show the crowd.

"Just to make sure it's the same coin, you don't have it anymore, do you?" the magician asked the child.

The little one's fingers uncurled, and sure enough, to the gasps of everyone watching—"It's empty! I just had it!"

"No, she did! And now it's mine again. Thank you, thank you." The magician took a bow, his hands spread wide in each direction, and several people made their way to the front to place coins in a clay pot near his feet.

Halleli and Hadar floated away down the path again before he started another trick. "That was fun," said Halleli.

"Definitely!" said Hadar. "I like getting the chance to see magic like that, instead of Isaac's stuff back at the palace. Something about wizards feels, I don't know, elitist to me. I mean, that purple guy? Anyone could learn those tricks, so it feels different."

"I know what you mean," said Halleli, "but technically, anybody could learn to be a wizard too. Not that I really know anything about it, but both the man back there and

Isaac probably got where they are by practicing a lot."

Hadar stuck out her hand and swung her body in a semicircle around the slender trunk of a carpentaria palm as they passed by. "Yeah, but the work's different. I mean, anyone can practice the kind of sleight of hand and tricks we saw back there, but to do what Isaac does you have to concentrate. You know I'm not cut out for that. I couldn't be a wizard, but I bet I could do the coin trick if somebody showed me."

"That's true, but that doesn't mean *everyone* could do the coin trick." Halleli bent down to remove a road rock from her shoe. "There are probably people who'd have an easier time with the thinking type of magic than the coin trick. Like—if they had stiff joints and couldn't move as fast. Or don't like touching strangers."

Hadar chewed her lip thoughtfully. "I didn't think of that!"

"Wizards do act pretty smug sometimes," Halleli acceded. "That's probably a big part of why it feels elitist even if it's not, really." She didn't say anything about it because she didn't really know how, but she felt sort of—*glowy*, and also lucky that she loved someone with whom she could have such interesting conversations.

A second happiness joined the first as Halleli realized that she felt the pricklings of fresh inspiration. The street magician, with his exaggerated movements and flashy clothing, would be awfully fun to draw. Surely she could find a place for him in a visual story for the queen.

Bits of the conversation with Hadar floated into place like puzzle pieces as Halleli imagined a story about two magicians. One would use sleight of hand, like the one they'd just seen, and the other would be a wizard like Isaac. Whose magic would win?

Her eyes widened as she realized the afternoon had just handed her the perfect story idea for her project for the queen. Who needed *male* wizards and magicians when there were witches in the world?

A street performer, using ordinary tricks, and a witch with magic spells. There would be mistrust at first, perhaps conflict, but then—a common purpose—and through it, love?

Common purpose...

Halleli's idea curled up in a ball and went back to sleep. Well, that was normal; she was used to these things coming in unpredictable and uneven waves.

She took Hadar's hand and continued walking to the forge.

The clanking of hammers on anvils greeted their arrival, and for a few moments they stood there in the doorway hand in hand watching the men work.

Hadar peered around, then said, "He's the one who has it, but he looks busy." She gestured to a man with his back to them as he worked with his current project.

"Yes, you'll have to... wait a moment," he called back to her without looking. After another minute he turned around, the sun-hot metal shaft of a small blade clasped between his tongs.

Halleli loved watching blacksmiths quench their projects, so she felt a little thrill when she heard the sizzle of its plunge into the water. This was lucky timing.

The smith drew the dagger out of the water and placed it aside. "Now, then!" He wiped his hands on his apron and approached the two ladies holding a folded paper. "You're lucky this didn't fall into the fire. This isn't the right place for games."

"Yes, sir. I'm sorry, sir," said Hadar, slipping noticeably into her Royal Guard posture. "Thank you though. We both appreciate it."

"Nn," the smith grunted in lieu of "you're welcome." "Tell the captain I said hello."

Hadar nodded briskly. "Yes, sir."

Halleli felt like she had a weight on her chest—she never wanted to be a bother to anybody. But just as they were about to turn and leave, the blacksmith seemed to relent slightly and winked at her. She smiled and looked at the floor.

Halleli still waited until they were back outside to do anything about the paper in her hand. "I'm sorry you had to go through all that trouble," she said as she squeezed Hadar's arm affectionately.

"Hey, I know you like to watch the quench."

Halleli unfolded the clue. "'The king who sleeps but never sleeps.' Whoaa... I have no idea, but I really like the way you said that!”

Hadar’s arms shot up in exultation as Halleli continued musing.

“King… well, we don’t have a king right now because Prince Kaveh’s just a Prince-Consort…” Halleli was speaking of Queen Shulamit’s political-only husband, who lived with his male companion on a vineyard outside Perach’s borders. “We haven’t had a king since King Noach died. Oh, this is about King Noach, isn’t it? Sleeps, death…”

“I guess it’s an obvious one,” said Hadar, “but I have no shame.”

“Never sleeps.” Images flashed into Halleli’s mind and she turned to Hadar, wide-eyed. “Are you saying something here is *haunted*? By the dead king’s spirit? We—”

Hadar’s mouth rose up in a grin. “No, no. Wow, you are, like, seventeen times more creative than I am."

 "I should write about dybbuks," Halleli whispered, half to herself.

 "He would never be something like that!" Hadar protested. "He was a good king."

 "Oh, I know," said Halleli. "But you said *never sleeps—*"

 "He's still with us in some ways, right?"

 "On the mosaics in the palace, you mean?"

 "What else?" Hadar pressed.

 "Old coins from before he died?"

 "Think bigger. A lot bigger."

 Finally, Halleli understood. "*The statue!*" She grabbed Hadar's wrist and took off toward the square.

 The monument to the late King Noach ruled over the Plaza of Moses on the far west of town, just before the docks. He faced the river, ostensibly in greeting to those who entered Home City by water. Halleli craned her neck up at him as they approached him from the south, looking up beyond the stone steps and careful plantings to observe his familiar face—bald to the back corner of his head, but then hair to his shoulders, and the bushy eyebrows he'd passed on to his daughter. "Look at the craftsmanship on his tunic," she breathed in admiration. "It looks like real fabric!"

Hadar reached out to touch it, as if to check what she knew to be true against her eyes, as Halleli continued her circle of the statue. Now that she could behold it more fully from the front, she saw that the king was holding a child in one arm, resting on his hip. It was a representation of the young queen, as she'd been at perhaps four or five—that was clear from the braids—but she'd been carved in a different style from the king. The little girl was roughly hewn, all right angles and sharp edges, as if the artist hadn't had time to finish her.

 "Because Shulamit's reign had only just begun when this was commissioned," Halleli realized out loud.

 "Wow, that is *deep*," said Hadar.

 Halleli looked up at the little girl, then at the arm holding her. She was afraid if she told Hadar what she was thinking that she'd hurt her feelings, especially after all this work she'd done to cheer her up.

 "Love?" Hadar could always tell though.

 "My parents have no statue," said Halleli in the tiniest of voices.

 "Oh, *love*." Hadar wrapped her in both arms and scrunched at her with one hand.

 "I know this is silly, but…" Halleli breathed in and out slowly, stopping the urge to cry. "They were so good and wonderful in so many ways, but nobody knows about them."

"Then you'll have to change that," said Hadar, continuing to rub her back. "With your pictures and stories."

"They deserve a statue."

"*You're* their statue." Hadar pushed her back slightly so that she could grasp both of Halleli's upper arms and look into her eyes. "You were created to honor them. You're made out of everything good about them, and you're standing here, just like Noach is, to watch the sun over the water."

Halleli smiled through tears. "The idea makes me feel better."

"I'm telling the truth! I'll even find some birds to poop on you if you don't believe me." Hadar patted her lightly with her fingers. "Plop! Plop! You're a statue."

This made Halleli giggle and sniffle. "Sorry."

"It's fine! I miss them too."

Halleli rested her head on Hadar's shoulder. "Where's the clue?"

"Oh! Right. It's under one of the bushes near his feet."

As she rooted around in the dirt, Halleli asked, "What will we do if someone else took it first and threw it away? Since you didn't leave it with anyone this time."

"If we can't find it I'll just tell you the clue myself."

"Oh! Here it is." Halleli shook it out over the soil, then unfolded it carefully to make sure stray bits didn't fall on her simple linen dress. She read out loud as she sat down on the top step of the statue's base: "'You can travel without bags, or horses, or a carriage. You can spend time in the distant snows without a coat; you can ride over the sea without leaving dry land. You can meet Miriam and Queen Esther and the Empress of the Mermaids, without getting out of bed or moving the cat off your lap. And what's better—you, my love, YOU can send people on these journeys. All thanks to this little object.'"

She'd been confused by the beginning, her mind pulled in all sorts of exciting directions by the horses and snowdrifts and sea crests of the clue. But when Halleli reached the end, she was smiling broadly, her eyes smarting with quite a different kind of tears from before. "That was really pretty," she blurted as she looked up at Hadar.

Hadar just did one of her little dances, then reached out and scooped up both Halleli's hands in hers. "It's the truth." She pulled her up and danced her around in a circle.

"The clue's at the bookmaker's, then?"

"Very good! If she hasn't sewn it into a book already."

"I'm sure she's put it somewhere safe," said Halleli.

"Look!" Hadar pointed to the docks. "They're unloading a ship."

"Ooh, let's go see!"

The girls hurried across the square to the street that ran parallel to the river, stopping short to avoid a couple of horses. "We'd better not get any closer; we'll get in their way," said Halleli.

"Can you see anything?"

"Not yet."

"Look!" Hadar pointed. "I think it's carrying textiles. There's Ben the tailor, from the palace. And those two women are also tailors."

"Oh," Halleli breathed in delight as one of the sailors unrolled a bolt of shimmering, red cloth for the Perachi customers. It shone with the richness of wine in the late afternoon sun. "It's so beautiful. I don't think I'd even be able to wear it. I'd just want to look at it."

As Ben and the other tailors negotiated with the sailors, Hadar and Halleli departed, walking along the riverside street. Halleli's eyes were almost entirely on the row of ships and boats, soaking in the inspiration for future projects. Her magician and witch for the queen's romance needed a quest, and quests usually required travel. Maybe a voyage by ship could be involved; then the women would be thrown into close quarters.

They turned left when they got to Flower Street, away from the river and into a ritzier part of town. "Oh, wow, all kinds of fun stuff in here," Hadar pointed out one shop, marked *Curiosities*. In the window they saw a wine goblet clasped in a dragon's paw made of metal, a lamp that looked like a water lily with a vessel inside where you put the oil and wick, and a huge pillow sewn to look like a violin.

 "That one's my favorite!" Halleli pointed to a glass-topped table held up by a metal octopus' eight arms and big, bulbous head. "It must cost a fortune."

 "You're right, that *is* one of the best," said Hadar. "You should draw it! Then you could take it home without having to pay."

 Halleli said nothing as she stared into the shop, memorizing the stormy curves of the beast's great tentacles.

 "Thanks for doing all this for me," she finally said as they continued their walk to the bookmaker's. She squeezed Hadar's hand.

 "Getting any story ideas?"

 "Lots," said Halleli, "I don't think I'm ready to talk about it yet though."

The bookmaker was sewing pages into a binding when the two girls arrived. "Oh, good!" she said emphatically as she stood up. "I was scared I'd have to close up before you got here. But I'm still working on this last set of Haggadahs."

"Can we see?" Hadar asked.

The bookmaker handed them each a finished copy. Halleli opened hers to a random page. *Had He satisfied our needs in the desert for forty years, and not fed us on manna, it would have been enough. Had He fed us on manna, but not given us the Sabbath, it would have been enough.* Dayenu.

Had He given me two loving parents, and not also a loyal wife to cherish, it would have been enough. Had He given me a loyal wife to cherish, and not royal help when the trees failed, it would have been enough. Had He given us royal help when the trees failed, and not delivered us into this beautiful city... Dayenu, thought Halleli. Her daydreams were richly colored and throbbed with energy as if alive, and she overflowed with religious gratitude.

"Ooh, is that Miriam?" Hadar pointed to a picture in hers.

The bookmaker nodded enthusiastically. "My sister draws those, when she has time."

"Halleli draws too!" Hadar announced, which made Halleli's cheeks flush.

"Oh?" said the bookmaker.

"Yes," said Halleli. "Come eat at the Frangipani Table some time, and if you pay extra, Chef Yael lets me sketch your portrait."

"I might just do that! I had no idea," said the bookmaker. "Here's your clue, by the way."

"Thank you," said Halleli, trading the Haggadah for the clue.

"This is the last one," said Hadar once they

were outside again.

 "That's all right," said Halleli, smiling shyly. "It's already been amazing. 'You couldn't drink this no matter how hard you tried, for five hundred million days. But you can float on it, and drink little things instead.' Float? Are we going back to the river?"

 Hadar shook her head. "Too busy. Think more private."

 "Quiet Lake?"

 Hadar nodded rapidly.

 "What kinds of little things?" Halleli asked.

 "You'll find out when we get there!"

 Hadar took the lead when they arrived at Quiet Lake, approaching the boat rental. Halleli thought she heard a fragment of uncouth humor between the two young men at the counter, but as soon as they saw the two women they stopped talking and played innocent.

 Hadar clearly felt like being brazen today. "What did you say about the one about the dancer and the two jugs of rum?"

 The man on the left burst into laughter, while the man on the right played the fool. "I don't actually know," he said. "I thought there was a joke like that, but I can't remember it now."

 "I can't either, then," said Hadar. "You still have that picnic basket from earlier, or did you eat it for us?"

 "We wouldn't do anything like that!" said the man on the right. The man on the left simply produced the picnic basket with a huge smile on his face.

 "Thank you! Here's the rest of the money I promised you. Now, where's our boat?" Hadar looked around at the water with her hands on her hips.

"That one there." The man on the left pointed.

"Sure you don't need us to come out there with you?" asked the man on the right. "Not as much fun when it's only girls."

Halleli wanted to disappear inside her hair scarf, but Hadar shot right back with, "Yeah, but we're *women*."

The man on the left chuckled and punched the other man in the side. "Stop being a kidney and go help them, or I'll tell Ima about, you know, the thing, with the girl, and the..."

"Shut *up*," said his brother, and went to go untie the boat.

Wow, thought Halleli. *Hadar could have said 'I'm in the guard!' Or 'Stop that, or I'll tell Captain Riv what you said.' But she just did that all by herself, without using her uniform or scary boss as a shield. She's the best.*

Hadar had the picnic basket, and she handed it over to Halleli once Halleli was seated in the rowboat, so that she could herself sit down. They pushed away from the shore and drifted out into the gentle waters.

"Thank you so much for today," said Halleli. "My soul is fed."

"Now I need to feed your stomach," said Hadar. "Open it, open it!"

Inside the picnic basket were: bourekas, roglit, falafel, chewy dried bananas, and tiny bottles of wine. "It's our whole dinner!" Halleli exclaimed.

Hadar nodded. "I got permission to do it this way. They're not expecting us at the dining hall tonight."

"So we can just relax in our room." Halleli sighed happily. "I think I've figured out my idea for the queen's art story now."

"Tell me!" Hadar bounced slightly, and luckily it was a sturdy boat so nothing bad happened.

"There's a beautiful witch in a shiny red dress, like that fabric we saw at the dock," Halleli began, "but also a woman street performer, who does the sort of magic that isn't really magic. Like the man in purple. They're on a ship together, arguing about whose magic is superior, but then they have to work together to go on a quest for magical treasures across the world."

"Like my clues!" Hadar realized.

"And of course they fall in love."

"Because that's why the queen is paying you," said Hadar.

"Well, because it's what *I* want to write," said Halleli. "Let's face it, if it didn't make *me* happy, do you think it would be any good in the first place?"

"So whose magic is better?" asked Hadar, her mouth full of falafel.

"It doesn't matter," said Halleli, rubbing her foot against Hadar's ankle affectionately. "They're both much stronger when they work together."